T0164619

THE FALL BEFORE THE RISE

ABHISHEK MUKHERJEE

PARTRIDGE
A Penguin Company

Copyright © 2013 by Abhishek Mukherjee.

ISBN:	Hardcover	978-1-4828-0031-9
	Softcover	978-1-4828-0032-6
	Ebook	978-1-4828-0033-3

Partridge books may be ordered through booksellers or by contacting:

Partridge India
Penguin Books India Pvt.Ltd
11, Community Centre, Panchsheel Park, New Delhi 110017
India
www.partridgepublishing.com
Phone: 000.800.10062.62

ACKNOWLEDGMENT

With all the love that I have in my heart, I wish to express my gratitude to those around me who have made this journey possible:

To the three most wonderful women in my life—my mother & my sisters for being so patient and supportive and believing in my dreams! As I always say, there is no *me* without *you*.

To Archana Aunty for tirelessly encouraging me! For always being my first reader & first critic!

To my precious family of friends—Kartik, Sudhanshu, Akanksha, Shruti, Rahul, Surya, Manjusha, Chaitra & Adi for your never ending support.

To Aditya Kumar (Adi)for helping generously with the pictures.

To everyone at Partridge Publishing for getting the boat to the shore!

—Abhishek Mukherjee

CHAPTER 1

Money can't buy happiness—a strong philosophy, even more strongly endorsed by my father, Surendranath Sinha.

Surendranath Sinha was a Government employee, having worked in the shabby confines of the Post office for the last thirty years. He was an ardent endorser of the middle-class. He took immense pride in introducing himself as one of them. He was one of those people who are never scared or intimidated by the rich. One reason for that was because he thought only the one without money or rather excess of it were the ones with morals and principles. Money was the root of all devils to him, so as to say. The other reason, I always thought, he could never know in his entire life what it was like to be living a life of comfort and opulence.

He spent his entire life in the small city of Kanpur; sorting envelopes and parcels within the confines of the four walls of the dingy post office. I remember how I resented going to the post office every afternoon with his lunch box. The place always smelled of old papers and glue. I would see old and unhappy faces everywhere. The typical frown of discontent writ all over these familiar faces! My father's office was even more depressing. The dimly lit room was littered with old files having gathered dust over the years and looking all set to gather some more dust probably for the next twenty years. There was a broken almirah with the words CONFIDENTIAL plastered all over it. The lever of the lock was broken and I don't think there was any effort to keep the confidential content it housed confidential!

Although to be honest I didn't know the meaning of the word. Thought it had to do something with confidence. I never bothered to ask and he never bothered to point!

His work station would always be full of receipts written in illegible handwriting, and old files and stamps and glue! There was no computer obviously! You wouldn't really expect to see one in any Government office at that time. Then again, computers I thought at that point of time were used only by scientists to make machines that would fly through time and space!

The room was always dimly lit by a 60 watt bulb hung right from the middle of the ceiling. Even at twelve in the noon; it seemed to be late evening. Time seemed to have had stood still for eternity in that room!

Anyways, my father was generally very happy to see me bring him his lunch every day. He would talk animatedly about a new stamp that might have been released or show me a new set of post cards with pictures of Eiffel Tower on it.

My father never collected stamps, but he made sure I had a healthy collection of these holiday-destination post cards. I used to collect them in my grandmother's old jewelry box. There was never any jewelry in that box actually! I would take them out of the box every night before going to sleep and look at them. The postcards, not the jewelry! They all seemed to be from some other world. The Eiffel Tower, The Leaning tower of Pisa! I was particularly fond of the Buckingham Palace. I had created this story in my mind about the princess caught in the Dark Towers of the Buckingham Palace and I liked to see that particular post card often! Sometimes there would be people, very pretty people posing in these post cards. And I would stare at them blankly for hours, wondering where they lived, what their life was like, what was like to be rich and happy! I always got the feeling that my father experienced a particular sense of pride every time we faced financial crisis and he would be able to steer us out of it. I don't think he ever borrowed money from anyone; he was too proud a man to do that! The legs and sheet theory was always high on his list of principles.

My father never allowed himself the chance that every man deserves to make his life better! I could never fathom how he was so content with life! We always lived a life of restraint and window shopping. Not only had he limited his own life but he was happy to deprive his two children of a better life they deserved. I could never complain that he turned a blind eye to our needs, because he didn't! To him, our needs started with education in a government school, graduating from a vernacular college and for me ended with probably getting married to a government employee earning two lakhs an annum.

The place where I grew up was mostly colonized by conservatives and may I add fairly middle class people. Middle class not only in their standard of living, but also in their thinking! They couldn't think beyond their limitations. I had never heard of anyone who stayed in our colony and made it big in life. Of course, these people would beg to differ. They would argue that Dimpy who now stayed in Dubai after marrying a chemical engineer had seen it all. Dimpy was the sole heir to the Queens's Showroom of electronic goods.

Queens' was owned by the extremely fat and potbellied man called *Lala*. I am sure that was not his name but everyone called him that and I called him *Lalaji* too! Lala was the richest man in the

4

Ranipur Society. He had everything or so I thought at that time. He had a beautiful house, a leather couch, drove a Maruti Esteem, his kids went to an English medium school and his ugly wife was always laden with gold jewelry. I hated Lala's wife though! She treated all the other women in the society like filth although she looked and was pretty much a cheap and lose woman!

Surendranath Sinha was a man of weird logic at times! I was four years old when he introduced me to my Guruji Pandit Haridas Chaturvedi. My father had apparently harbored the dreams of becoming a classical singer but he couldn't! Guruji always joked he sounded more like a mule when he sang! Anyways he wanted to live that dream vicariously through me! So there I was, when children of my age were busy getting hurt falling down from a tree or swinging on a tire, I was sacrificing my childhood so that my father could live his dream. Although I didn't understand any of that, I was too young and my father kept on playing like an old record that this was for my own good!

Did anyone ever ask what I wanted? No!

Did I question anybody? No!

Why? Because I was taught that people from good families do not ask questions when asked to do something.

So it was not until a few years back that I learnt that ignorance is not always bliss after all! And that you don't get answers unless and until you raise the questions!

I was born October 28 1987 in one of the general wards of the corporation hospital in Kanpur to a 23 year old mother, Savitri around ten thirty in the morning and my father decided to start pushing my luck from exactly eleven o 'clock by christening me Bittu Kumari Sinha, a baggage of a name I had to carry on my weak shoulders for the first many years of my life!

Do I resent my father for naming me mindlessly? No! Actually I am glad he didn't just number me or name me after one of the city post offices! Though I am sure I have heard of a post man in his office called Bittu! But I didn't have a choice and I have seen many a variety of expression on people's faces when they hear my name for the first time!

Times have changed in the last few years and so have I. I have by choice shed the chrysalis of the past and embraced the new me! I am no more Bittu Kumari Sinha but I suppose I am not embarrassed by her anymore! Bittu has given way for Maaya! And this is a story about the journey of Bittu and Maaya—a story of the games people played with them and of the games they played with them!

*   *   *

CHAPTER 2

The early 2000s was the era of change. Y2K, the year was supposed to bring doom to Earth, deliver its Nemesis! People in Ranipur Society kept on talking endlessly how they have seen on television the skies would come crashing down on humanity and robots will take control of who so ever remained alive. But thankfully none of that happened! That's the beauty about myth. They never are true and also they awaken deep primal instinct—paranoia!

Speaking of paranoia, my father was never a huge fan of the cable TV. He was, like most other, was of the opinion TV is indeed the idiot box and the cable the idiot savant! There were constant arguments between him and my mother. While my father argued how it would spoil me and my brother, my mother argued on the lines, she at least wanted to see what the rest of the world was like, even if it meant through TV. Though he didn't buy that argument, the *chulha* strike at my house the next day pretty much sealed the decision in my mother's favor. And soon we welcomed cable TV into our hearts and life with eager anticipation!

And as it turned out, my father was right! I was completely enamored by the beauty of the cable tv. It was like opening my grandmother's jewelry box, only a hundred times more pleasing to the eye. Everything was catching my attention, the places, the people, the glitz and the glamour. TV became my window to a whole new world. I started realizing how much was I missing out. And though logic suggested that everything you see on TV is not true, but I guess logic loses steam when you are a teenager and you feel trapped!

There were a couple of shows that had completely captured my imagination. First it was the cult show—*Kaun Banega Crorepati*, a quiz show hosted by Amitabh Bacchan. And second, a show called as *Sa Re Ga Ma Pa!* It was a show where singers, from across the country gathered to compete for that recognition and of course, the money! This show was considered as the gateway to Bollywood. Many a talented singer had made that stage their own and had gone on to win the hearts of a billion people. The show had produced gems the likes of Sunidhi Chauhan and Shreya Ghosal!

And before I realized something strange had happened! The show had gotten to me. I couldn't get enough of it. I used to enjoy the show thoroughly. And there was a reason to that! I had started relating to the show, to the stories of the hardships the participants spoke of on the camera. I bought every one of them. I didn't have a favorite. I liked everyone. They were all me, it seemed! I would be thrilled if someone got a good comment from a judge and absolutely miffed if someone sang well and still didn't get enough points. There was an attractive romanticism with all the hardships the contestants faced in their life and how they had decided to stick to their dreams despite that! It was the ticket to the good life. And now I wanted that ticket!

I would stay awake all night wondering how to get out of this place! I was convinced this was what I wanted. This was *my* ticket out of there! But I didn't know how to go about it. I spoke to my mother about it. I thought she would be angry. I even had a convincing speech ready for that! But then, what was I thinking. She laughed it off, thinking I was getting cranky and acting abnormal because of my periods.

"You have gone mad!" she said laughing on my face.

"What is there to laugh?" I asked, obviously not amused.

"You really think they are going to let you on that stage?" she asked, still laughing.

"Why? What's wrong with me? I am a good singer and I know that!", I said trying hard to keep my voice down.

"Listen Bittu! This is not for us! People like us have more important things to do in life, much more responsibilities to take care of. We don't have the money and the time to spare on a wild goose chase!" she said blatantly without looking at me, flipping the chapatti on the *tawa*.

As I looked at her that night, I realized it was pointless arguing with someone who had spent her entire life washing clothes and cooking food arduously but without a complaint! She had resigned to her fate. And she never thought I was going to have a life any different than hers! Watching her that evening, I felt hapless but at the same time resolute about my decision. I was not going to waste my life!

But I was not sure how was I going to get out of there. I was getting frustrated and my father noticed it. Our middle class standard of living had suddenly started embarrassing me. I was getting conscious of it by each passing day. I would keep staring at myself in the mirror. I started hating my oily hair, my big ears, and my gawky tall body. I looked like an ostrich to myself. I was constantly conscious of what I was wearing. And hated going out with Dimpy's younger sister, Mona, Lala's youngest daughter.

We used to frequent the movie theatres often. She always had enough money to pay for the auto rickshaw fares, buy the popcorn and eat *dosa* after the movies. But off late every time she offered to pay, I would get irritated. It seemed to me that she was trying to prove I was poor and I was her bitch.

She was a pretty girl and all the money and comfort gleamed through her face and her expensive, branded clothes. My self-esteem took a hit every second I spent with her. The boys would speak to her and not even look at me. She would talk to them in English and I felt she did that intentionally knowing I couldn't speak in English. And even if I could, why anyone would talk to me, I thought! I was a post master's daughter, wearing *salwar kameez* stitched out of my mother's old saris!

It's funny how caustic jealousy can be! We are blind enough to misjudge others and push them to the point where they actually become aware of things about us that would irritate them. I did exactly that.

Mona had noticed the change in my behavior and let alone Mona, any gold fish would have had the brains to see what it was about!

When you see a poor little stray dog on the road, if you are a kind hearted person, or at least trying to be a kind hearted person, you feed the creature with some biscuits. And how it latches on to each piece! You try comforting when it looks scared and doesn't want to come near you. You scratch its head and back, not caring about the little ticks on its body. But soon it gets used to the regular supply of food and love you provide and why would it not! He doesn't have to search the trashes for the same. Also it becomes the sore of the eyes for the rest of the stray dogs because you give him the biscuits and the attention, just because he had a small little limp! And then the ungrateful in the dog starts to surface. One day you forget to get the packet of biscuits, he starts tugging on your favorite skirt and you don't like it one bit. You shoo it away but the dog thinks it's your job to get him food and shower him with love. It starts barking, showing off its ugly teeth. And you don't like him anymore. Suddenly you start wishing you had a clean, well fed, trained pet dog. And then you stop paying any attention to the stray dog. It barks for a few days when it sees you, probably to vent its frustration or maybe longing. But soon it starts realizing the ship has sailed and it is back to being where it belonged. To the low and the dirt!

Something of the sorts happened to me! Mona tried to figure out why I was feeling like this but my problem had become too deep seated to be uprooted by mere talk or a promise of another movie at the Ragini Theatres. And soon one day, she lost her patience and showed me my place.

It was straight out of Hindi film. She invited me to her birthday party and then in front of all her richer, cooler friends asked me to leave her house because apparently her maid servant dressed better than me. As a matter of fact she did.

"Here take this you tramp! "She said as she threw a five hundred rupee note on my face. "And go get some clothes and a prettier face! And before you spend the money, show it to your father, who probably doesn't even know what a five hundred rupee note looks like!" The laughter of her friends echoed in my head.

The fury, the anger was burning my guts inside but I stood there hapless allowing the tears to dry on my face. I will never forget that day, because that one night had changed me forever. I had known what I wanted to do, but somewhere I didn't know if I had the stomach to do it but when your fears subside the heart takes a strong stance. In my case, my ego had been battered, and my resolve melted the fear.

Had I known though, how much would I regret it in the days to come, I would have been careful but I was hurt and I was ready to bear the consequences. And consequences I bore!

* * *

CHAPTER 3

My dignity badly bruised, it was getting difficult by each passing day to spend more time in my house. I would start feeling breathless and claustrophobic and would run up to the terrace. But it was not my body, but my mind and heart that were feeling restless and trapped. Even sitting under the open sky on the terrace would not take away the restlessness. It would rather make it worse. From the terrace, as far I was concerned, I could only see two things now.

Lala's posh house at the end of the street! How it stood tall amidst the rest of the locality! The glamour and captivity that Lala's house adorned so gracefully would make all the little houses around it look like the ruins of an ancient civilization. Not that they weren't actually! Ranipur Society was an artist's painting gone bad. Most of the houses were not painted, so they all stood in the skeleton of bricks and cements with discontinued construction of a floor on the terrace. And the ones that could be called painted were somehow holding onto the last traces of them, like an old lady not willing to take off her bridal dress.

And I often wondered what our house looked like from Lala's terrace. I was certain that Mona would take her friends to the terrace, show them my house, and make fun of it by calling it a hut! The more I thought about it, the more I would seethe with anger.

For days, I was preparing the grounds to approach my father to let me go to Mumbai. I knew one of his sisters, a cousin, stayed there. And I heard stories about her being rich from my brother!

Every day I would pack his lunch, sometimes even making it, and took it to his office with a forced smile on my face. Not only that I would sit there till he had finished it. I was sure that all my loving would somehow soften him up and he would let me go to Mumbai at least once.

Finally after a month I gathered enough courage and decided to tell him one afternoon. I made his favorite *gobi paratha* and took it to his office. I waited till he finished his last bite, wiping the little traces of pickle left in the lunch box with the last morsel and licking his finger.

"Baba, do you think I am a good singer?", I asked hesitantly.

Baba looked up. He was surprised by my question.

"Well, of course, you are! Guruji is always praising you. He keeps telling everyone that Sinha's daughter is the best student he has ever had!"

"Baba, I want to take up singing seriously!" I paused and then started again, clearing my throat, "I want to go to Mumbai!" My heart skipped a beat the moment I said the last sentence. But Baba's reaction to say the least surprised me.

"But what is the connection between your singing and Mumbai?" he asked genuinely after a moment's pause of trying to add the two up and evidently failing to do so.

"I want to participate in a singing competition . . . on television!" I said clearing my throat further trying hard to drive home the point.

Baba kept quiet for a moment, this time it seemed to have made more sense to him.

"Do you even know what you are saying? Do you think it's a joke? Do you realize its actually not that pretty as you see it on TV?" he said, his expressions become grave with every word.

"But Baba"

He didn't let me finish.

"This is the end of discussion. I am not going to let my daughter get into this kind of mess!" and he walked off.

It was not the end of discussion.

That night we had a huge fight. Until that night even I didn't realize I had become so adamant about going to Mumbai. Every time he said no, I felt he was murdering my dreams. And I couldn't bear to take that. I was convinced I wanted to get out this place. I hated the mediocre life. I was sure Mumbai would change my fortunes. The more Baba disagreed with me, the more magical Mumbai seemed to me.

I kept on arguing until my mother slapped me for raising my voice against Baba. And one would wonder I might have wet my pillow crying that night. But I didn't. I didn't shed a tear. Because no matter what my parents said, I was going to Mumbai.

It was a matter of time and now it was time to figure out how!

Luck has a funny way of playing with us. It stands at the end of the road and lures us. And makes the road leading upto it look so rosy and picturesque. You imagine there would not be a single thorn to slow your stride and when with all the confidence you put your best foot forward, you realize that things are not the way you imagined. But then by the time you realize you might have made a mistake, you are too far down the road to turn back. And you decide to embark on a journey full of hurdles, thorns, heartbreaks and of shattering perceptions and dreams to get to where you had set out for!

*   *   *

CHAPTER 4

A few days after my heated discussion with Baba, I saw the first glimmer of hope.

There was a cultural gathering organized during the festival of *Makar Sankrant.* Anybody and everybody who knew a bit of singing or dancing or had any other two bit talent were asked to put up a show for the people of the society. And naturally, I had to take part in this monkey circus because Baba wanted me to. I did it every year and I detested the prospect of doing it again.

Not only I felt it was a waste of time as no one appreciated anyone's talent; the gatherings were usually repulsive because there would be drunken men losing their balance everywhere.

So one would wonder how this was a glimmer of hope for me? Here is why!

The gatherings were usually organized around *Sankrant* time. The festival was not the sole reason for organizing it. It was more because Lala's brother in law, Harry would visit his family every year during that time. Of course, Harry was a derived form of his original name Harish which he had dropped when he went to Mumbai.

Two things happen when you have never seen the world that breathes outside your cocoon. One—anyone who comes from outside seem far cooler and superior to you and two—you are pretty much in awe of whatever they say.

Word was that Harry was the owner of a big event management company in Mumbai. Whenever he would visit our locality, people would treat him no less than a celebrity. And he would court everyone with his anecdotes about meeting different Bollywood stars. He would even carry a small photograph in his wallet. The one with a bearded Bollywood super star!

So obviously every time he visited Ranipur Society, people found it an obligation to treat him on par with Prince Charles. Again I am sure half the people there didn't know who Prince Charles was, so chances are Harry would get a better taste of hospitality than he would, at least in Ranipur Society.

But then again, when you have had seen so less of the outside world like I had at that point of time, things appear far more attractive to you than they actually are! So although Harry pretty much looked like a pimp with his gaudy floral printed shirts and kitschy tight pants, accessorized by his lose golden watch and pierced ear with a diamond sitting there like a peacock in a pile of crap, I was in awe of him. More so this time than ever before! And no! I have to point out, even though I was at hormonally active age, I didn't have any sexual inclination towards him.

I was sure though, that Harry could be the one who helped me out of Ranipur Society. Come on! I had every reason to believe that. The man had had breakfast with many a famous star. So perhaps, he could use his resources and contacts to get me on one of these talent shows. At that point, all I wanted was an opportunity and I was convinced, it would be a different, albeit a much comfortable, life for me form thereon.

* * *

I was seeking opportunities to speak to Harry. Baba was not particularly fond of the man, though he never suggested why. He found it distasteful the way Harry would keep the two buttons of his shirt open to show off his bristly chest. Not a pleasing sight to an aging, orthodox man, you will have to concede!

My recent tiff with Mona did not help my cause either. I knew I couldn't speak to him anywhere near her. Because I was certain, she would leave no stone unturned to sabotage my plan. And I had to do some ground work before I could approach him. I couldn't just walk up to him and ask him to hold my hand and take me to Mumbai. Could I?

Looking back, it pretty much turned out that way.

But much on that later!

My first encounter with Harry was the morning of the Sankrant festival. As usual people had gathered on their rooftops for the kite flying competition. My brother, Dev, was pretty good at it. So despite me having no interest in it, I would always help him with the *manja*. And this year, I made the *manja* sharper than any other year. I wanted Dev to beat Lala. I was sure seeing Mona on the losing side would be of some comfort to me. And despite me hurting my hand quite a few times, I didn't mind it, as long as Lala was losing.

As we got on the terrace I saw Harry on Lala's terrace. He was speaking on his mobile phone. I was looking at him and when he saw me, he smiled back. It was very nice of him, I thought! At the same time I saw Mona and was convinced she would have said a word or two about me to him. It didn't occur to me, to her I was garbage and people don't talk about trash to their family! But I wanted to keep feeling important and I did!

The next two hours was intense with the entire locality screaming at the top of their voices. All sense of semblance was lost, as neighbors jovially hurled abuses at each other for damaging their kites. But my brother was a perfect picture of calm and composure. He has always been like that. Nothing fazes him. It's as if he always knew where he has to get at or reach and no matter what, he will! I envied that about him. He occasionally came across as extremely boring because he always played it safe but even playing safe is a strategy. It requires patience and mental strength. And only those who are clear about their goals can afford to play safe!

And here too, he played safe. He kept his kite at a safe distance from the rest of the crowd on the sky. He waited patiently as he let others to lessen the crowd. And then he started going for the kill when there were only a few left. With almost magical dexterity he made one kite after one fall from the sky and gather dust on the roads. And then it was him and Lala there up on the sky.

Lala went in for the kill. People cheered. Dev swayed to the left. Lala chased him. Dev turned a sharp left. Lala had him corned and everyone cheered again. I started feeling nervous. I looked at Dev. He just returned a smile. As calm as the fish in a turbulent river! And then Dev soared and Lala chased him up. Deva soared and soared until the kite started looking like a spec in the sky. It was getting difficult to look up in the sun. And then it clicked me. Dev was waiting to blind sight Lala. Brilliant!

And it worked like a charm! Dev took his kite almost vertically upwards till the sun was directly in our eyes. It was impossible to keep looking up. And then Lala faltered. He reached to wear his sunglasses. Dev who was playing deer all this while turned into a predator. He seized the opportunity. He dipped and took one last sharp turn and before Lala could understand what was happening, cut him across. There was a moment of silence as everyone paused to appreciate Dev's brilliance and they all erupted. I erupted and ran downstairs to collect the fallen soldier. I was going to put its corpse up in our living room.

But as I turned into the narrow lane beside Mr Shukla's house to collect Lala's kite, I realized I wasn't the only one in that empty darkened nook. I turned behind to see Harry was also running for the kite. Harry was not that old. Actually he was fairly young. He must have been twenty nine to thirty by what I measured. Patches of baldness made him look middle aged.

I was running hard but he was catching up on me. And the lane was so narrow there was only space for hardly a man and half another to run side by side. Soon he was running so close to me that I could feel his breath on my shoulders. And then he was so close to me, I could feel his body brush against the back of my body. I didn't know whether to feel offended or given the circumstance, just let it pass. I mean, we were both crammed for space. Then somehow he managed to squeeze past me forcibly towards the kite. And in the process did something that had a chill running down my spine. This was the first time since I was fourteen when one of my classmates Tinku had done something like this. I giggled the last time, not so much this time.

Harry in an effort to squeeze past me pressed his chest against my breast. And stood there for a moment! Almost as if enjoying the feeling! Of course, Tinku was not so much discreet with his attempt. He had used his hands to feel me up at the end of school one day when we had both stayed back to finish our homework. And while I didn't mind that, of all my awe of Harry, I didn't feel quite comfortable with this.

Noticing I was a bit paralyzed by what happened and the ensuing thoughts that engulfed me, Harry took the opportunity to pick up the kite. It was when he winked at me wickedly and smiled, showing off his tobacco stained teeth and pan-painted tongue that I realized I had to get the kite. I saw him walk away with what was going to be my prized possession.

And I decided to momentarily to let the small incident that just happened take a back seat. I wanted to get the kite. Not only it was mine, someone else was walking away with it. I couldn't let that happen.

So I followed Harry. And just as he was about to turn the end of the nook that led to the open main road, I held his hand from behind. He turned to look at me. I smiled coyly. I held his hand, he smiled back but he didn't let go off the kite.

And then a side of me surfaced for the first time. A color of mine that I had never seen myself! Obstinacy is a state of mind and is completely circumstantial. When you constantly keep getting denied of anything you want, you crave for anything within your reach. A want metamorphoses into a temporary obsession, an obsession that you are not going to let go until you get it. And that' what exactly happened with me! I was being denied of a life and I was sure of that! And suddenly I felt denied of one more thing that I wanted. The kite was no longer a kite. It stood for what I wanted. It was my cake and somebody else was going to have it.

And then the cunning in me surfaced!

When I realized he was not getting to let go off the kite, I knew I had to divert his attention. And although I was seventeen, I knew men have a short attention span when someone of the opposite sex is giving them the slightest of hints or opportunities.

And indeed his attention faltered!

*   *   *

CHAPTER 5

I leaned on to Harry slowly, my body brushing against his! I could feel his breath getting heavier. I was waiting for the moment when he would loosen his grip on the kite. I still held on to his hands and leaned a bit more on him bashfully.

I bit my lips to portray and exaggerate my actual excitement which was next to nil and to also paint his imagination with me feeling coy! Harry's back was resting against the wall and now my body was completely brushing his up! I could suddenly sense his mind and I knew I had to act quickly. Suddenly, he let go off the kite from his hand, and I wasted no time in taking hold of the coveted kite.

But at seventeen you are immature and stupid! And looking back, I have to admit this was stupid, not because it made me look cheap but also because every action has repercussions. And I had under estimated it this time. To this day, I wonder what if my mind was not that obstinate, what if the cunning in me had not surfaced that day!

Maybe I would not have had to endure what I was about to endure. But then again, beyond every dark night the sun rises. And I was sure the sun would rise on my life too!

Let me talk about the immediate repercussion.

Having got hold of the kite, I was about to turn around and leave from the scene. But what I hadn't realized was that there was a reason Harry's hand had let go off the kite. He had slipped his hands on my waist. And that I had not realized until I turned around, started pulling away from him and felt the tug.

His hands clasped me tightly, pulling me closer. It shook me up. I saw into his eyes directly and this was the first time, I knew the look of lust. Honestly, until that moment in my life, I was not sure if any man would ever want to come near me. I was not pretty and I was not rich! The latter a more significant reason to me than the former!

And going by that logic I should have felt flattered and wanted. But I did not. No girl likes it when some creepy pimp-like guy stares down your shirt.

But then, to be honest, I had led him on. It was not entirely him. I had pricked his lecherous instinct.

But Harry had his mind somewhere else. Suddenly, he was staring down my flimsy cotton kurti. And he kept on leaning forward on me, until he was pressing his body completely against mine. Lack of self-respect or presence of mind, I don't know what, but I didn't do anything. I felt helpless. I felt over powered and worst; I didn't know what to do.

And then suddenly, he let me go. He gave a smile and let go off my hand. It was like he was toeing his feet to see if the water was warm enough. Apparently, it was not warm enough yet. But the look on his face said it all, as I walked away nervously from there, adjusting my dupatta to cover up my exposed neckline. That sooner or later, the water was going to be warm enough for him.

Call me cheap, call me naïve, but as I lay on my bed that night my mind had already started scheming something. Our desires can all so often spin a web around our logic and lure our ever-believing heart into the trap. In this case, my mind was spinning the web not only for my heart, which I must say was already convinced about the scheme. But was also scheming to spin a web around someone else's heart and mind!

Yes! No prizes for guessing, it was obviously Harry! But looking back, had I known Harry a little better, I could have saved myself from the trouble of thinking so much.

The next few days I tried to radiate as much charm as possible. Notice I say "as much as possible". The reason I say it because at that time, I was plain ugly. And the way I used to dress up or carry myself didn't help matter much either. So as much I could I did.

I made it a point to go to the terrace so that he could see me drying my clothes. Or walk past his house to get the daily groceries, knowing he was there on the balcony. I would look at him, smile and just keep walking on. He would just smile politely, bob his head and keep staring.

But somehow we didn't get the chance to speak much for a week or so, apart from exchanging pleasantries and stealing glances.

I had never stepped outside Ranipur Society, so although it has been difficult, I have managed to forgive myself for being so stupid. When I spoke about spinning a web around Harry, my idea was to just smile at him every day, be coy, exude my charm, and if possible, have another of those covert and clandestine incidents that we had back in the alley.

All because I saw him as my ticket to Mumbai!

I had heard so much about Harry's connections and networks in Mumbai, that I was convinced, he could give me the opportunity I was so craving for. The human mind is weird. It just cannot act smart when the need be! And I paid the price for it in the days to come.

But then one day, as I was going to Baba's office with his lunch, I saw Harry waiting outside the house with his luggage, hugging and saying goodbyes to his family. I stopped in my track. Mona was there. She saw me staring at Harry and gave me her daily dosage of dirt. I couldn't care less.

Harry was leaving. I had forgotten he was visiting all but for a few days. I felt disappointed for strange reason. And I walked off. I turned around as I kept walking and I saw Harry's eyes following me. I wanted to talk to him but I knew I couldn't. The feeling of helplessness was making its comeback and indeed it was! More so, because I knew once he was out of Ranipur Society, it would be impossible for me to be in touch with him and I would have to wait for another year, if at all he returned.

*　　*　　*

CHAPTER 6

Destiny has strange ways to bring you closer to it. And I had entered into a phase of my life where I was destined to go through certain experiences.

As I was sitting outside Baba's office with his lunch box, I noticed what seemed to be Lala's car stationed outside the post office. I got up and went closer to the car. I saw the driver was changing the rear tire which was flat.

"Bittu?", I heard a familiar voice. A voice I knew but I couldn't recognize at the moment. I turned around and saw Harry standing behind me, in his usual floral printed beach shirt and tight pants, accentuating his paunch.

But that's just what my eyes saw and my brain didn't register. What my heart saw was my glimmer of hope smiling like an angel, having appeared out of nowhere like a tooth fairy.

I stammered to say "hi!"

"You look nice today!" he said.

I almost giggled.

He looked at me almost as if measuring me.

"I didn't know you were leaving today!", I said, every word dripping in disappointment.

"Something came up in Mumbai. Needs my attention!" he said almost non-chalantly.

I allowed the word "Mumbai" to linger in the silence for a moment, savoring every bit of excitement that it brought with it.

"I am going to be back for Holi though!" he said breaking the silence.

"Oh! That's in a month!" I blurted out.

"Yes in a month!"

My hope was rekindled. All was not lost yet.

"I would like to see more often when I come the next time around!" he said with a smile.

My heart skipped a bit. "Harry wants to see *me* more often! No one wants to see me more often!"

I allowed a giggle again.

It would have been safe to assume that I was falling for him. But then again, it's easy to get confused why was I falling for him. Did I actually like him or was I just looking at him as my meal ticket? Who knows! I was too young to differentiate. I was used to people snubbing me. I was used to people not calling me by my name around the civilized and here he was, not giving a damn what my name was and he wanted to see me more often! Over the moon would be the right phrase to describe my elation at that moment.

"I would love that!" I said when I finally said!

"I think you should go!', he whispered. "People are staring at us!"

And yes, they were staring at us. "They are just jealous I thought! I am talking to a rich man who has this big a car!" I thought to myself.

But then I didn't want to be the talking point of the locality and I didn't want any of Baba's so called well wishers to tell on me. So I just left already counting the days to Holi. And in the meantime also forgot to give Baba his lunch. That was just the beginning of me being in my world. A lot was yet to come.

That night as I took out my grandma's jewelry box the romanticism of the post cards appealed to me on a different level. I could picture myself in one these, wearing expensive clothes and shoes I didn't know where I could buy them, standing next to a rich and handsome man, in front a historical monument which I didn't know on which part of the world it existed, if at all!

The next few days I was lost in my own world. Every morning I would wake up and stare at the calendar which my father used to get every New Year from the post office, keeping track of the date and day. *Holi* was marked in red, as like the other festivals and holidays.

My daily ablution time had gone up. I would spend hours standing in front of the mirror, staring at myself and wondering what would I look like with a bit of make up on. I would pretend people hovering around me for my autograph and dying to get a picture clicked with me.

I didn't spare the morning newspaper too! Didn't matter to me which part of the world was bombed by the Al-Qaeda or who was winning the election. I would go straight to the fifth page of the hindi newspaper, because that was the glamour page. I would picture myself being featured with a huge picture of me in my last night's performance, with an extended interview at the bottom of it. I would practice the answers. And most of the time, I would talk about how I was poor and ugly, and then fine day, an angel walked into my life and showed me what my life could be. The interview would always end with me giving a motivational speech to the youngsters and dreamers out there to keep chasing what they wanted and not to give up on their hopes.

I really started believing that I was one of the few who could dream and go onto live the dream.

The funny thing about the jewelry box was it was like my heart. Every time I would open the box, I felt I was opening my heart, opening to the idea of possibilities. I would drown myself in the imaginations of a grand life that I wanted so desperately. And the moment I would close the box, the mediocrity of my life would come to bite me. Every time I closed the box, my hatred for my life, my family and my house multiplied.

I couldn't stand the sight of me in the mirror. My own ugliness was getting to me, my middle class clothes was tearing me apart and above all, the thought of having to spend a listless, meaningless life like my mother scared me! No, actually it disgusted me!

I had made up my mind. The coming Holi was going to bring about the change in my life. I was going to snatch the colors and paint my dreams with them!

When the heart decides, there's not much the mind can do!

CHAPTER 7

One of the few good things about Ranipur Society was that it celebrated together. Be it Dussehra, Diwali or Holi the people in Ranipur Society would make it a point to enjoy the festivity together. It always irked me! I couldn't ever fathom how they could be so happy and celebrate with so much zest, where did they get the strength to humor themselves, despite being neck deep in debt and struggling to make both ends meet. Naturally, I used to keep to myself during such times, willingly trying to avoid the general merriment.

But this Holi was different. I was going to make it count. I was waiting for my time. I couldn't wait for the day to come. The anticipation had started making me restless and unmindful. My grandmother at one point of time started wondering if there was any disorder called as extended PMS.

Harry arrived the night before the Holi. I was standing on the terrace collecting the *papad* my mother had left to dry there. I saw a blue sedan parked outside Lala's house. I waited for some time to see if it was Harry's. It was not the car which he had got the last time. This car was bigger and shinier. I knew it had to be his.

I went downstairs to see if my mother knew anything.

"Amma, did you see the big car outside Lala ji's house? ", I asked casually.

"Yes, why? she replied.

"Nothing! It's a new car. Is it Lala's?"

"Don't be silly Bittu! His wife spends every penny on decorating herself! Doesn't spare a change for him! It's Harish's car, he came this afternoon!", she said covering her mouth to avoid the smoke from the chulha entering her mouth.

"Oh!", I said trying to sound as casual as possible.

"Hmmm . . . he has come with his wife this time! Wonder how he managed to get such a pretty wife!"

"Wife?", I almost shrieked.

My mother was taken aback by my reaction. I obviously didn't know he was married.

"Yes, why?"

"No nothing! Didn't know he was married, that's all?", I said as I turned back my attention to her.

I saw her looking at me.

"What?" I asked. "Why are you staring at me?"

"You have been acting strange the last few months! You seem to be lost somewhere! I really don't know what's going on inside your head!"

"Oh come on! Don't start now! My mind is where its supposed to be!", I said as I walked out of the room, forgetting to give her the stack of papads.

She waited for me to remember. I went outside and switched on the tv, the papads still in my hand. It was when I tried to pick up the remote to change the channel; I realized my hands were occupied.

As I went inside to give her the papad, I saw her shaking her head. I thought she did have a point. I just smiled and left.

*   *   *

The next morning I woke up with a strange feeling of excitement. After a very long time, if not the first time in my life back then, I woke up looking forward to what was ahead of me. I also woke up with a bit of headache cause the loud speakers which was put around the locality for playing the music during Holi had woken me up. Catchy Bollywood songs were being belted out at the highest decibel levels and as I went to the verandah, I saw the kids had already taken to the street, playing with color, running around shirtless, chasing each other with plastic pistol guns filled with colored water, in their hands.

As I came out to our small living room, the sweet smell of jalebis wafted from across the kitchen, where my mother was making the sweets for the guests. It was one time of the year, my father did not mind spending a bit.

"you better change into something dispensable", my mother advised.

"its almost ten o clock and people have already started playing colors. Don't start yelling if someone marches in the house and paints you like a rainbow!", she said with a grin.

"In fact, we would be going to Lalaji's house in a while!", said my father, without looking up from the newspaper.

"We are!", I said, not knowing why my heart had started beating fast at the sound of that.

"What's wrong with you? That's where we go to play Holi every year, like everyone else. Although he has cordoned off the lawn this year! Your brother had made a mess of it last year!"

I quickly went inside to check on what I could wear. I wanted to make sure I looked nice. Actually, I wanted to make sure I looked desirable to Harry. The talk about him being married had completely escaped my mind. Maybe I had allowed it to!

I picked up a white salwar kameez which I thought fitted me well. I spent the next half an hour inside the bathroom, standing in front of the mirror, putting on kajal and practicing to smile coyly. All for the flutter of a heart!

An hour later, we finally went to Lalaji's place. The place was already bustling with uests. There was so much noise and loud music that it was difficult to hear anyone talking. The men had taken to the bhang like fish to the water. The jalebis were adulterated too, with powdered bhang.

Out there in the lawn, which was supposed to be out of bounds, the air was filled with colored cloud. It was hard to differentiate one from the other. The faces were painted with weird combinations of color and the only way I could distinguish who was who was by the way they were behaving, After all these Holis, I knew exactly who would speak what after a two glasses of the bhang spiked thandais.

My eyes however were searching for someone else. It had been fifteen minutes since I had walked in the house and I hadn't seen Harry. Then suddenly I felt a tag on my hand from behind and before I knew I was drenched! For a moment, I thought it was Harry. But I was disappointed. It was Mona!

I completely looked over the fact that she had put her differences with me aside and was behaving so jovially with me. She tried putting color on my face but I resisted. Don't know why! It was holi, the festival of colors for crying out loud! But I gave in. All the memories of our childhood came rushing over me and was enamored by the beauty of nostalgia in no time.

We were like the old friends again, hugging each other, dancing in the loud music, playing with color. I was enjoying every drop of water that was directed towards me. My mind had completely wandered off from Harry. But just like that, I started feeling out of breath as I saw Harry on the terrace. He was smoking and looked visibly high. Mona saw me staring at the terrace.

"Lets go up there!", she said pulling my hand.

I was confused.

"It will be fun throwing water from up there on the people down here". She had missed the fact that I was staring at Harry.

I didn't say no! Hell! Why would I have! The very purpose of going there was to meet Harry and in the darkest corners of my heart hoping that some sparks fly between us.

As we went up to the terrace, Harry's back was facing us. He didn't notice us. He had his arms around the waist of a woman, his one feet on the wall. She was his wife. I saw her the first time when she turned around, unknowingly becoming conscious that somebody was standing behind them.

My mother was right! She was too pretty to be Harry's wife and like my mother, the first thing that came to my mind was how did he get a woman like that! But it didn't take time for me to add up two and two! Of course! He was rich! That was about it.

I felt conscious of myself being around her. I forgot all about playing color. She was elegant, pretty and amidst all the hue and cry going around, she looked like a picture of a calm sea. She had the perfect figure and her skin glowed in the soft spring sun. It was evident she came from a rich family but there was something about her face that gave the impression that she was radiating power.

I was looking for ways to avoid having an eye contact with Harry in front of her, there was something intimidating about her. Thankfully, Mona was high on the bhang. All of a sudden I heard a huge splash of water. She had already started pouring water over the people in the lawn. And in a moment of frenzy turned around and splashed an entire bucket of water on me and Harry's wife.

The moment she did that, she knew she had made a mistake. Harry's wife was far too classy for this kind of childishness. But she held back her scream. She just gave her a disappointed nod of the head and walked off from the terrace. Like a scared and wet cat, Mona followed suit. I could hear her sorry echoing as they went downstairs.

I instantly turned around and found Harry standing right behind me. And before I could say anything, he held my waist and pushed me against the wall. My heart was racing fast. He slowly grabbed hold of my waist and pushed himself on me. It was happening all too fast and he was so close I could only see his reddened eyes and feel his body on mine.

"Oh! I have missed you!", he whispered in my ear as he felt my neck.

I was going week in my knees. I had never felt such a sensation in my life. My body was shivering. It was hard to tell why. Maybe because I was scared that someone would see us.

I somehow managed to gather my wits and push him away a bit.

He looked a bit confused. Almost disappointed! I obviously didn't want him to let go off him completely. I was waiting for a chance to tell him to take me away to Mumbai! And then he said something that was hard to avoid.

"I will make all your dreams come true!", he said in a soft, seductive voice. I wanted to be sure he was talking about what I was hoping for.

"What do you mean?", I asked timidly.

"You think I don't know what a fantastic singer you are and how badly you want to get out of this place!". I was amazed. I had never told him anything.

"How do you know that?", I asked carefully.

He almost guffawed at that.

"I know how to read eyes dear, and your beautiful eyes have so many dreams trapped inside them!".

I could have sworn I was in love with him at that moment.

"I could give you everything you want, everything that you crave for, every opportunity that you have longed for!"

Now it was my turn to play along.

"And why would you do that?", I said not having a clue what his intentions were. Rather let me rephrase—didn't have a clue as to how far stretched his intentions were!

"Don't you know that!", he said leaning forward on me again.

I didn't say anything, trying to fathom how deep had I got myself in! It was one of those moments I didn't know whether to feel guilty or not! I wanted him to say exactly what he wanted.

"Listen here!", he said pushing me again. He was not talking to my face anymore. His eyes were fixed somewhere south from there.

"You have turned into a very attractive girl! And you . . ." he paused to take a look at my face once!.

". . . Are", he continued as if allowing every word to sink in with me and, "going to give me what I want!".

It shook me up. All this while I was silly enough to presume that a bit of flirting is going to convince him. I had stepped in the den and I was pretty much stepping on the tail, I realized!

"What?", I asked not wanting to hear what he was dying to say.

He stepped back a little bit and smiled, I could sense, at my naivety.

It seemed he was trying to get the right words to put across what was going on in his mind but then he went for the simpler, more honest option.

"You!"

The immaturity of the heart sometimes does not allow you to weigh your options to figure what are the consequences of our actions and decisions. There is no way to explain what I was trying to achieve through Harry. The man didn't strike right at the first go with anyone and yet I found myself smiling when this disgusting looking man said he was going to make my dreams come true. If I fell for that, and the blind ambition of my heart, I deserved every day of my life that was about to come then on!

* * *

CHAPTER 8

I went home not knowing which path to take, the one which told me to break all contacts with Harry and find my way on my own, or the one I was promised if I held his hand The second road had a few obstacles but seemed guaranteed.

"One night, that's all!" I heard myself saying.

"One night and my life would change for the better!"

I had to take a decision and I had to take it quick. This time I couldn't afford to waste any more time. The next time, it could be a long wait.

I got up from my bed to look myself in the mirror. I kept staring at myself, my face, my hands, and my body. I realized how conscious I had become of my looks. And then my eyes fell upon something. In the reflection of the mirror, I saw my grandmother's jewelry box.

And the next thing I knew, I had made up my mind.

Standing in front of the window that faced lala ji's house, I picked up the phone and dialed Harry's mobile number. I could see he was smoking on the terrace.

I knew everyone at his and my house was in an inebriated state; the bhang having done its work.

The phone rang. I saw him get up and take the phone out of his pocket. He stared at the screen. Didn't recognize the number! I waited for him to answer. After allowing it to ring for some time, he finally answered.

"Your place, in 10 mins!", I didn't even let him say "Hello!'.

He kept quiet for a moment. He didn't know I could see him—a bit confused, almost as if trying to recognize the voice.

"Bittu?". He asked cautiously.

"Is that okay?"

His expression changed completely. He started rubbing his chest. And with a toothy grin he said, "of course! Just remember not to ring the doorbell. Enter from the back door and come to the room in the terrace!"

I hung up.

I should have been shaking, one might wonder, after making that call! But I was not! On the contrary I felt strong, having taking the first decision of my life. This was my life and I was willing to change the way it was.

Since the time I could remember, I would feel that life had been unfair to me. And always ended up staring at the heavens, shaking my fist in anger and asking why He couldn't make sure I was born in a rich family!

I wanted to have a life! And I was not willing to wait around and find out if someone was going to give me that. So I decided to snatch it. I didn't want to ask for it anymore, I was ready to make the deals!

I quietly stepped out of my house with everyone sleeping. Going by the intensity of their snores, I was sure I had at least two hours in my hand to come back without anyone even realizing I was not at home.

The only person I was wary of though was Mona! I didn't want to run into her! Even after her treating me nicely that morning, my resentment towards her had not mellowed to say the least. Her bursting into flames was a wish I still garnered.

Of all these years of having played hide and seek at Lala's house, this was the first time I was entering his house through the back doors. I knew the entire architecture of the house, so getting to the room on the terrace without catching anyone's attention was not a big ask from me! Not that I needed to be so cautious. Loud roars of snores were resonating through the thick walls of Lala's house. I could have entered with the entire orchestra playing and they wouldn't have known.

I carefully closed the door of the terrace behind me and peeped through the door of the room in the terrace that was half-cracked open. I saw Harry sitting on the bed with a glass of rum in his hand. I pushed opened the door and stood there for a moment as I saw him looking at me. I could see his eyes looking at me, though my clothes. It was the look of a hungry animal. There was something disturbing about the look. It didn't feel right.

But I knew it was too late to turn back! I didn't have the strength to turn back. Somewhere deep down, I didn't want to refuse what was going to happen; all my dreams were hanging on the clothes covering my body.

At this point, I had started hating myself. I just wanted to get it done with! I tried to picture my dream again! Me on a stage, with the spotlights on me, people cheering for me, chanting my name, the thunderous applause resonating in my ears

He grinned at me, having a gulp of the rum, his eyes fixed upon me.

I hesitated. Stood there again for a moment before I took a step forward! That didn't go down well with the impatient bastard!

"Come on! Don't just stand there or you want a little help!", he said with an evil wink, showing of his disgusting set of teeth.

"Half an hour! I will get what I want!" I was coaxing myself.

I was getting conscious at the thought of every piece of clothing that was about to come off from my body, fear engulfing me with the idea of every inch of my body starting to surface.

My heart started beating fast; not from excitement but from the anxiety and the fear with every glance I stole at him. He was smacking his lips. His tongue, pan-stained and of freakishly red colour!

He was ugly and I couldn't believe he was going to have his way with me. I was going to let him on me. He was always a big, bulky man, the kind of people you see on the *before* slide on weight-reduction clinic advertisements. His tummy looked the size of a boulder and the mere thought of him being over me, scared me.

"I am going to die!" I said to myself. And i was confident I would!

I took a deep breath and slammed the door shut behind me.

*　　*　　*

"How old are you?", he asked all of a sudden lifting his head.

"Why do you ask?"

I almost broke into a giggle.

"Just answer me, will you?" I loved it, he was on my mercy!

"I'm nineteen!" I said nonchalantly turning my head towards the right. My eyes fell upon a fruit knife on the ground, must have fallen from the table!

My mind had wandered off to the huge cupboard kept in the room. *Definitely teak wood,* i thought to myself. The shiny knob, the clean mirror on the wooden frame had my attention. I imagined the clothes it must have housed inside, and the jewelleries! I saw myself sitting in front of that mirror on the foot high chair, trying to wear a big rock of a diamond on my nose. The intricately crafted earrings; the smooth fragrance of spring beaming in pride each time the doors were parted. The platinum bangles intertwined each other on my hands, jostling for the spotlight that could win my heart!

Oh! Orgasmic!

The late afternoon sunlight was met in between by the few lonely, travelling clouds. The result was a shade of sepia seeping through the room, kissing the shiny white marbled floor.

After a couple of minutes, he lay down next to me, gasping for breath! His gleaning sweaty body made him look like a pig. The traumatic few minutes lasted lot lesser than I thought it would. He didn't know much about pushing the envelope.

"Look at you, so young and untapped!" he spoke finally.

Untapped! What was I, some kind of coal mine!

"Yes! I have kept to myself!" I said.

"You are like a dead—frog!"

"You glad you did a corpse?" I asked, my expression stone—dead.

looked even more disgusting as he lay there stark naked, without even making an attempt to cover himself up.

I managed to get up from the ground somehow, my legs still feeling a little weak. It had more to do with Ray's over weight frame than anything!

I felt something sticky at the back of my thighs. There was blood on the ground and for the first time since the time I had entered the room, I felt embarrassed. Don't know what it was, but the blood on the floor reminded me I had sacrificed something huge here. Everyone wants to remember their first time as something special, but as I walked towards the bathroom to get cleaned, I quickly realized that this was something I would love to forget as soon as possible. Then again I knew I was going to live with it forever.

I just didn't lose my virginity that day, I sacrificed it. I mortgaged it to get something back, to get my life on track, to live my dream. And no matter how much it hurt physically, my mind was calm and my resolve stronger.

I came out of the shower after a quick shower with my clothes on. I didn't want to show any inch of my body to that man again! I knew he used me, but I did the same thing!

"You are quite a bitchy little thing!", he said with a wink.

"What the hell? Keep your shit to yourself and talk business now!" I clearly didn't have the stomach to listen to his nonsense anymore.

"Woah!", he said as he got up with a jump. My reaction had taken him by surprise.

"We just had some fun, didn't we?", he winked again.

His winks were now irritating me so much I could have stabbed him in the eye ball had I found something near my hand. I saw the knife on the floor.

"Listen Harry! You got what you wanted; now I want a word on what I want!"

He got up to light a cigarette! He put on a robe which hardly covered him up.

"So what is it you want me to do?", he asked looking surprised.

"I want to become a singer. I want to participate in shows and I want you to take me to Mumbai and shape my life!"

He laughed out loud at this point; again, I am sure at my innocence, or whatever was spared of it.

"You think it is all so simple, is it not?" He kept on laughing loud. At this point I was scared; someone would wake up and walk inside the room!

"Mumbai is a scary place Bittu! It will eat you up! And who do you think I am! I couldn't waltz into some studio holding your hand and ask them to make all your dreams come true because I fucked you!"

"But you did fuck me saying you will take me to Mumbai!" I almost protested in a voice choked with tears and fear!

At this point, I was crashing into million pieces inside, but somehow managed to hold myself together in front of him. I tried to hold back the tears but it did trickle down my cheek!

"Oh don't cry Bittu! It is silly! You had a good experience, didn't you! I will take you to Mumbai if you want, be together, have some more fun like today! But I can't promise you I'm going to make you a super star! How can i? I am simple man after all!"

I couldn't figure why he had that wicked smile on his face. The more i looked at his face, the more devilish he looked. And the more naked I felt. I didn't feel this naked even why I lay there on the ground. But despite all the clothes, I could feel the nerves of my broken heart! Poking me like a broken barbed wire stuck under the feet!

I stood there for a while, trying to gather myself together! And then it clicked me. I did hold back one card, didn't i?

"Harry, you WILL take me to Mumbai and you WILL make everything you can to use our contacts to make sure I get my opportunities!" The resilience of my words took me by surprise too. Though it was hard to measure his incredulity!

"Listen here! Now you are irritating me! Just get your head together and get out of here! I don't want you to get into trouble."

"If I were you, I would be worrying about my troubles now, honey!". I said as I slowly walked towards him.

He waited for me to continue. He sensed I was quite serious.

"Which year is this Harry?" I asked as I frisked his robe playfully.

"2004! Why?" I could see he was trying hard to figure where this was going.

"Right you are! Let me give you a fun fact and then a simple calculation! I know you are not that bright but every *baniya* worth his salt can at least figure this one out!"

"First the fun fact: Bittu Kumari Sinha was born in the year 1987!". His jaw had already dropped. But I continued.

"That makes Bittu Kumari Sinha 17 years old as of 2004 and may I add, more importantly, a minor! So basically, you fucked a 17-year old helpless, innocent girl, Harry!" I dramatized with a curled lip.

That was one time when the gaucheness of his own appearance was matched in intensity by the incredulity of his face. The smoothness of the whisky must have been feeling like the coarseness of the tar down his throat. And his breathlessness was evident by the way the little beads of the sweat were trickling down his forehead.

That was the day Maaya was born. Harry tricked me, consensually or otherwise, doesn't matter now! But I had my own plans and I had my own games. I was 17 and I had the life of a man hanging by the thread of my willingness to spill the beans. But then that was hardly my plan. If I did that the game would have been over. This was just the beginning of the rat chase and I had my trumps ready to be played in the times to come!

*   *   *

CHAPTER 9

There was an eerie silence that followed. I had clearly blown the winds out of his sail. By the looks of his expression, his mind had gone into a tizzy, thinking about all the possibilities that could go wrong for him now!

It took him a while to gather his wits. And then finally, his voice which had deserted him for a while came back again.

"But . . .", he paused again and this time not because he wanted to but there was a click of the door knob and before we could realize his wife, Mallika was standing in front of our eyes.

She stood there in utter disbelief and it was evident that she had heard our conversation. Also, looking at our appearances, it would not have been hard to guess what had preceded the conversation. His robe was half open and I stood there, with the clothes on but my look all disheveled. Looking back, I can only imagine what must have been going through her mind. I would definitely not want to be in her shoes.

"Mallika!" he shrieked.

She didn't say anything. She picked up the dupatta from the ground and wrapped it around me.

"Mallika!" He called her name again! I really didn't know what he was trying to do, not that I'm sure even he knew what he was going to do. There was a strange fear in his eyes, almost the fear of his life.

She took a few careful steps towards him and just stared at him. She didn't utter a single word. She conveyed a strange sense of calmness, and to be honest I was scared. I even looked at her hand to see if she had a gun or a knife in her hand. She didn't paint a picture of a volcano ready to erupt. But of an ocean ready to absorb anything in its way without leaving a trace behind!

"Get dressed! We need to talk! Get the car out now!". She said in a commanding tone. Harry didn't utter a word. He just started walking.

"Oh and Harry!", she stopped him in his tracks.

Mallika turned around and slapped Harry right across his face. I didn't see her slapping but only heard the thundering sound of her hand leaving a red mark on his face.

"Now make yourself scarce!"

At this point, I was trembling. My knees were shaking and for the first time in my life, I felt engulfed by a powerful presence. As she made me sit down on the bed by putting her hands on my shoulder, I felt more at her mercy than at I had felt under Harry.

"Are you okay?" she asked with what seemed like genuine concern.

I just nodded in disagreement. I was definitely not okay.

"Are you hurt?" It was a question that broke me down. Of course I was hurt, more at heart than anywhere else.

"You are Surendernath ji's daughter, right?" she asked.

I was embarrassed when I was heard his name.

I broke down, and covered my face with my hands. I was crying inconsolably.

Mallika helped me up on my feet. In every sense of the phrase! But for that moment, she just took me out of the room and helped me in the car where Harry was waiting.

"Keep driving Harry! And don't talk until you are told to!" said Mallika.

Harry carefully adjusted the rear view mirror and tried to catch a glance of his wife.

I could still the weight of my guilty conscious and Harry's overweight frame as I rested my back; the chill of the cold floor still fresh despite the warm leathery seats of the car.

"His wife! ". . . His wife!!!", it suddenly struck me, I had slept with her husband and she had been really calm about it till now! Now she was taking me away somewhere in the car. It didn't smell right! The first thing my pea-sized brain added was she was going to murder me in the car and then dump my body somewhere in the woods.

"Wait!", I screamed out.

She didn't look surprised. As if she almost expected it. Harry didn't turn back and look. He just kept on driving.

"Stop the car!" I screamed again.

"And you stop screaming!", Mallika replied tersely.

"Where the hell are you taking me?"

"I told you; we three need to have a talk and obviously that can't be done in that house!'.

"Oh! How convenient! So that you can kill me and dump me somewhere!".

She didn't look too pleased with that.

"You look here girl! I don't care what's going on inside that head but you listen to me carefully!" She was talking between her teeth. She was seething with anger but was too dignified to show it.

"I don't know why you slept with my husband or what motif you had but I know one thing! It has to be settled! And it has to be settled now!".

"What do you mean?", I was curious. She was starting to sound dangerous with every word she said.

"Is it true whatever you said about your age?", she inquired. I glanced at Harry. He was keenly listening.

"Don't look at him! Just answer my question! You don't have to be scared of this basterd!". Such contempt for her own husband, I thought, and yet she was trying to figure a way out. It was not making sense

"Yes!", I replied meekly.

"She lied to me, this bitch!", shot back Harry.

"You will do well to keep quiet! And anyways, I will deal with you once we get back to Mumbai. I am trying to clean your mess here, so shut the fuck up and keep driving!". Again, that stern tone had a dangerous overtone to it. Her composure was giving me goose bumps!".

And then my heart leapt a bit! Out of nowhere another disturbing thought had queued up in my mind. I had not paid attention to Harry putting on the rubber hat. I couldn't recollect him wearing one. But I let it go, thinking I must have missed it. I was hardly paying any attention to what he was doing, or trying!

"Did you lie to him?", her tone far more softer.

"Yes!", I replied sheepishly again.

"How stupid of you!", she said in a disappointed tone.

"You can't obviously be in love with him, that's for sure; any living creature which has undergone evolution can't be attracted to him. So just tell me, why did you agree to sleep with him?"

I kept quiet for a moment, trying to gather the right words that would make me look less cheap.

"how much money you want?", she asked non-chalantly. I looked at her in disbelief.

"Don't look at me like that! Just tell me how much you are worth to keep it yourself?".

"You think I'm some kind of whore?", I retorted.

"Your actions don't suggest otherwise!". She said looking out of the window.

Was she wrong in thinking the way she was! Of course not! I would have thought the same way and when she said it aloud, I did add up to that.

"I want to be a singer. I want to go to Mumbai! I want to showcase my talent on a big platform!" I said. How naïve of me!

"Let me guess. This prick here told you he is going to help you out if you slept with him?" By the looks on her face, she already knew the answer but asked nevertheless.

I nodded in affirmation.

"You silly, silly girl! You should know better than that! He is just a sleaze ball. He just goes hangs with a couple of people who claim they are producers but are actually bigger sleaze balls than him. And may I add he is their bitch! These guys are almost a bunch of pimps! They are not going to do anything, apart from you. But that goes without saying!".

I couldn't take my eyes off her. The sharpness in her voice cut through the silence in the background that was only interrupted by the sound of the car engine. I couldn't help but wonder what had I gotten myself in!

"So that's that? I sleep with this guy, sacrifice my dignity because I want to make my dreams come true and all you can do is humorously lecture me! You do realize that if this gets out, that your husband slept with a minor, where is he going?" It surely had to be a drowning man's desperation hat got me talking finally.

"Now you are talking!" she said. "I must say you played him nice!"

"Anyways, that's not the point here!" she continued, I was all ears.

"We are going to make a deal here; something that works for both of us here!" Harry had stopped the car. He obviously wanted to listen. He too didn't have a clue what his wife was going to offer here.

"If I want, you can vanish without a trace! That would never be a problem and all your blackmailing will go down the gutter along with your spleen and liver! But that's not the way I work! I believe in honor, and in protecting my family's honor; something that my father has earned after years of toil." The trembles were back in my knees. I was not dealing with a road side thug here.

"I'm going to take you to Mumbai and help you with whatever you want! You will have a life you wouldn't have even dreamed of! But I have two conditions." I was listening with bated breath. I had forgotten all about Harry. He seemed trivial at the moment.

"You will never talk about what happened this afternoon, never ever in your life! Not to your shrink, not to your friends over a drunken state, not to your future lovers in a state of orgasmic joy and not to your parents whenever you ever again get to re-unite with them!" The last bit took me by surprise.

"Re-unite?"

"That brings me to my second condition. We are going to leave tonight and you will be coming with us. You will not tell your parents about it. You will just write a letter, pack a bag and come with me. Tomorrow, you start a new life and the baggage of Ranipur Society will not be coming with you! Infact, you are never going to come back here!" She was looking straight into my eyes.

"Why must I not tell my parents anything?"

"You must pay too for your actions! Everything has a price! And trust me; you don't want to say no to me!"

I was dumb founded. On one hand, she was promising to be my tooth fairy and on the other hand, she was cold-bloodedly threatening me. Who was she?

Of course, I got that answer later. Much on that later though!

"Why should I believe you?" I asked although my skepticism was not clear to her. She looked at me in utter dismay.

"Harry took me for a ride! What if you are lying to me?"

"Look here Bittu", somehow gathering my name and giving a weird expression too, "we both have lots to lose here! In your case, everything! And in my case a lot of pride and goodwill. Not my husband, trust me! I would trade him for a donkey if I could!"

I would be lying if I said I didn't trust her. Every word she said, she said in a no-nonsense 'tone. I actually believed everything she said. I latched onto every word she said. My life was moving on to a new chapter and it was happening all so fast.

I had always thought of leaving the mediocrity of Kanpur behind and move to Mumbai. Mallika was turning a new leaf for me. She was writing a new chapter in my life. And somehow despite getting the feeling that I hardly had any say in it, I was more than glad to take it up. The thought of not seeing my parents surprisingly didn't bother me much. I must have been a horrible daughter. Thankfully, my parents didn't have to know what happened that afternoon and what was going on in my mind.

"I hope you are not going to decline the offer, are you?", asked Mallika.

I looked at Harry, looked at her. Mallika was not even looking at me. Harry was staring at me, wide-eyed. He must have been praying I declined the offer. It was a two way sword for him.

"Yes! I am ready to do this, but I, too, have a condition!"

"You don't have any!", she replied curtly.

I said it nevertheless.

"I don't want Harry to be around me, or try to take advantage of me! I don't want to live this nightmare again!"

She looked at him and said, "He will not as much come near you! If he does, he knows what price he will have to pay!".

Harry just turned around in the front seat and wiped his sweat. All my pre conceived notions about the man had changed right in front of me. From believing him to be the fulfiller of my dreams, to seeing him being treated like a pet dog, it was an eye opener that there is always more to it than meets the eye.

I was to shed the skin of my past that night. As I went home that evening, I saw my mother making tea for the rest. She was still groggy from the bhang in the afternoon. Baba was sitting with his head in the hand, a clear indication of his headache. And Dev, my brother, the only person in the family who looked at me like a human being and not just another head count, studying.

"Where were you? I was looking for you. I thought you were at Lala ji's house but Mona came looking for you." He asked.

"She did?". My heart skipped a beat. Had she too found out?

"Yes, she came to return your bracelet. She found it on the terrace!"

"Of course not!" I thought. I must have dropped it around the first time, not in the bed room.

I simply took the bracelet and walked off to my room. He was saying something but my mind had already wandered off to somewhere else. That was my last conversation with Dev for a long time to come. That memory of my family in the living room was the last memory of my family since that night for a long time to come. And that indifference towards what Dev was saying was the beginning of a long period of indifference to come!

CHAPTER 10

"Dear Baba,

By this time, you must have already noticed that I'm not home anymore. I have not gone to get milk or feed the birds at the lake. I'm gone! I have been trying to tell you what I want to do with my life but I couldn't help notice that it didn't matter to you.

It's not your fault that I dream big. But it's not my fault either that you dont! I want to have a life and living here in Ranipur Society was never going to work for me. I refuse to live a mediocre life. Maybe I will struggle, I know I will and even if I fail, I know I have tried.

I know you will hate me now, but I hope one day when I achieve everything I want, maybe then you will see the sense in it! Until then I don't feel the need to explain anything further.

—Bittu

I had walked out of the home with a bag containing three dresses and a five hundred rupee note that night. I walked till the end of Ranipur Society where Mallika and Harry were waiting in the car. As I sat in the car and closed the door, I closed a chapter of my life and embarked on a journey that few get to experience in a life time. Fear in my heart but belief in my dreams!

I hardly spoke during the journey. We travelled continuously for two days in the car. With every tree on the road that our car left behind, I was leaving behind a part of my life. With every bridge that we crossed, I was bridging the distance between me and my dreams. With every whiff of fresh air that blew through my air, I could feel myself breathing life into me. I had never seen the inside of a big car and now there I was but not a trace of excitement. The only thing I was waiting for was Mumbai, the *mayavi nagari, the city of dreams.*

Finally after two days we reached Mumbai. Mallika woke me up from my slender slumber.

"We are here!", she said.

"Where?", I asked still a little groggy.

"*Pratap Singh Bhavan*!", she replied beaming with pride.

"What's there?", I asked not having a clue what were we doing in a bhavan. I always related the word bhavan to Raj Bhavan.

"We are home", she replied patiently.

My eyes were on the brink of popping out. *Home!*

I glanced around from behind the carefully tinted window of the car. It looked like a different country. The car was parked behind three other cars, three other very big cars. The parking lane was cutting right across the lush green lawn on both the sides. I had never seen grass that was any greener. The sun was beating down but the air smelled different. It was the rich smell of opulence and of Mumbai! The sprinklers were watering the lawn, I thought they were magic water, coming out of nowhere from the ground.

I stepped out of the car carefully, not knowing where to look. Everything looked so different and beautiful. Anything that my sight fell on, I couldn't take my eyes off them. Even the way two big dogs were running and rolling around on the lush green.

"Come on in! We need to go inside. ", said Mallika.

"And listen!", she stopped me as I put my first step out of the car. "Baba is going to ask a few questions, DO NOT open your mouth, just nod along with whatever I say."

"Did I have a choice?" I asked myself. I just nodded in affirmation.

I dragged my light luggage and heavy foot across the lawns and stood at the door of Pratap Singh Bhavan; at the door of a new beginning of my life.

CHAPTER 11

The moment I walked inside the house, I felt as if I had stepped into one of the post cards in grandmother's jewellery box. The spectacular sight bedazzled me as I stood there in the middle of the hall with my jaws almost touching my feet. For someone who lived in a small room; was scared to get on the bed for the fear of having her head cut off by the ceiling fan, it was evident that the first thing that I noticed was the height of the ceiling, which to me seemed was almost hundred feet high. The inside of museums are perhaps less opulent and the furniture of the most artistically inclined beam with lesser pride as compared to everything that was there in the gleaming white room, mosaicked with utmost elegance and diligence.

Mallika gestured me to sit down on the couch, which looked so expensive that it made me uncomfortable. Had she asked me to sit down on the floor, I wouldn't have minded but the prospect of sitting down on the white leather couch made me extremely conscious. And the first thing that ran across my mind, what time of the month was it!

I reluctantly sat down, almost on the edge of the couch, trying to make the most minimal contacts with it. Two servants scurried out of nowhere, with glasses of water on a tray. I noticed they made a conscious effort not to make direct eye contact with Mallika when they exchanged pleasantries. Mallika was surprisingly polite to them and even asked them if they had had their morning breakfast. For some weird reason that eased my nerves!

"Baba will be down in a minute,", she said looking at the flight of stairs, which gave me an eerie impression of the stairs to Heaven!

My eyes fell upon Harry, who was constantly wiping the sweat streaming down his forehead.

He was not even looking at me. He looked like a lamb who knew he was to be slaughtered but the uncertainty of whether or not meeting his fate this day, was writ all over his face!

But I was too over awed by the décor of the house for his pale face to hold my attention for too long. This time my eyes had wandered off to the strange looking coffee table. The glass frame rested on the most magnificent piece of wood work I had ever seen; a crouching leopard! The brilliance of it to me was not only its uniqueness but the careful carpentry which detailed every curve so magnificently that it looked like it was just waiting upon its prey!

My meditation with the coffee table was brought to an abrupt end by the sheer intensity of a laughter that filled the room suddenly.

I immediately looked towards the flight of stairs. And almost reflexively I stood up on my feet.

"Welcome back! Welcome home my love!", thundered the man walking down the stairs. I felt the chandeliers would come crashing down.

Mallika walked over and gave the stylishly grey-haired man a hug. He was dressed in a khadi kurta and was wearing a long white beard and an even broader smile on his face. This surely had to be *Baba*.

Mallika went over and hugged him; no such emotions from Harry though! He grew paler by each passing second, stealing glances at the man and trying not to look him in the eye.

Pratap Singh was by no means a common man. And it had nothing to do with his wealth. One look at the man and you could figure Mallika had his genes and where she inherited the blue-blood pride from!

As for me, instead of being intimated by him, I was intrigued by him. I had not met too many men of significance in my life earlier. But I guess, I was definitely somewhat close to what can be described as being in awe.

"And who is this?", he said looking at me.

"She is Bittu!", that's all Mallika answered.

I politely folded my hand and said Namaste. Pratap Singh reciprocated with a courteous smile. And he turned towards Harry.

"Namaste Baba!", he said from a distance. He was sweating profusely.

"What is the matter with you? Why are you looking so pale?" asked Pratap Singh, turning his attention to Harry, trying to get the measure of him.

"Nothing", stuttered Harry. "Just the long journey!"

Pratap Singh did not look interested in him anymore.

"Anyways, I have lots of work to do today! The campaigns start in a week. So we better not waste any time!" he said turning to Mallika.

"Be in my office in half an hour!" he said as he started climbing those stairs again.

"I will be there in fifteen minutes Baba!", said Mallika.

She turned towards me and gestured to follow her. I picked up my bags and started walking behind.

"Leave those behind!". And she marched ahead.

I dropped the bags and scampered behind her. At this point, I didn't know what to make of her. I wanted to trust her. I wanted to believe that I had made a new beginning to my life. I wanted to believe that she was going to make my life better. And as I dropped the bags, I wanted to believe that I had dropped the baggage of my past. But at the same time I was also scared. I didn't know what was coming next. The fear of uncertainty was creeping its way through my guts. And as I walked past Harry, I didn't feel anything. I wanted to believe that I had made a sacrifice that night for the life I wanted. And I was positive the price was already paid when I let that bastard run his tongue over me.

* * *

CHAPTER 12

I followed Mallika into her room. It was across the magical stairs. If the blue carpet on the stairs amazed me, I was yet to be amazed even more as I entered her room. It was a huge room and had i known at that time what the insides of a five-star hotel looked like, I would have thought it to be one. It was fascinatingly decorated. The bed was so huge and looked so comfy that I felt relaxed and sleepy just looking at it. There were at least four cupboards and I wondered what it housed! She was a woman of taste. It was evident from everything that was there.

Then my eyes fell upon a photograph of her and Harry together on the table beside her bed and I wasn't sure about it anymore. Maybe one of those bad decisions she might have made.

I waited for her to say something. She was sitting in front of a ten foot high mirror on the dressing-table; removing her bangles and earrings. I noticed the entire set of fancy make up kits that sat pretty there. And the fragrance of the room—it smelled like lilacs! It was nothing like the sweaty odour of our house.

And then she spoke; looking at me in the mirror.

"We don't have time to get fresh now! You can take your shower after we come back from Baba's office!". I nodded.

Why was I going to baba's office? But I dared not ask.

"Remember; don't talk until I ask you too! Just nod along with whatever I say!"

I was sure she was not going to tell her father her pervert husband had jumped me but I was not sure what was she going to say.

She got up and started walking out of the room.

"And one more thing! Don't talk to Arjun!", she said it with a hint of threat.

Arjun? Now who the hell is that! But I dared not ask!

As we walked out of the room, my body was hurting from the journey and I desperately needed a shower. I was feeling itchy and dirty. My hair looked like a mop and my clothes, well, they were anyways not worth talking about. Probably the sight of the bed had made me crave for comfort a little more.

But now we were going to Pratap Singh's office and I had no clue why was I being tagged along. It was hot and I didn't want to travel. But the thought of sitting in that big car and seeing the roads of Mumbai excited me.

But my excitement was short-lived. Rather it was replaced by another moment of disbelief and surprise.

I followed Mallika through the carpeted corridor to another part of the Bhavan. And as she knocked softly on the big wooden door, I knew this had to be the office.

We entered the room together, albeit in different styles. Mallika, obviously with a stride that said she belonged and me, well, another moment of amazement and trepidation! More like a wet cat stepping into a kennel to hide from the thunderstorm.

The room looked more like a library than an office. There must have been nearly a thousand books on the dark ebony shelves which were crafted on the wall. The room was painted bright white. And the center of the room was occupied by a huge desk with the pictures of Gandhi, Nehru, and many more prominent political figures hanging on the walls.

There was one picture of Pratap Singh with hands folded and an outlandishly huge and heavy garland around his neck. That picture told me the story of who the man was! Or atleast what he did! A green couch; where I saw a tall man sitting with his back facing us! He was engrossed in reading something.

And yes, the all-time favourite cliché! The room was filled with smoke. Both men were smoking their way to glory.

Pratap Singh looked a little alarmed on seeing me in his office this time. This office was a special place to him. And over the years, I came to realise that this was more like the lion's den and anyone whom Pratap Singh didn't approve of was not to enter the room.

He got up from his big chair and waited patiently for Mallika to explain. There had to be an explanation for her to bring me to his office.

"Baba this is Bittu!". Amidst all the names that were present in the room and the weightage they carried, mine seemed like a noise in the middle of an orchestral symphony.

"She is one of Harry's distant relatives!". I could have fainted had I had a chance to do that on hearing that.

Distant relative? Are you kidding me!

"And?", asked Pratap Singh not knowing what to do with that information.

"And she is going to be with us, if that is okay with you?"

"Is she is in trouble?", asked Pratap Singh with sincerity in his voice.

"Yes!", she replied.

I had no idea what was cooking in her mind at that time.

"Her family was marrying her off to a very old widower", she paused for a moment, and then added, "*forcibly*!", stressing on it. That pause she took was brilliant. It gave the entire fake story such life and drama! I almost bought it! And she was selling me!

"Well that's too bad! She doesn't even look like she is of legal age to be married! Are you *beta?*", he asked taking a step towards me.

I almost burst out laughing when he asked that. Even he could see that, but Harry couldn't. Though his libido had blind-sighted him, that's a benefit of doubt one could give him!

"Well of course not! That's the entire point. She is under-aged and poor girl doesn't even have a mother!"

My jaw dropped at that. *Doesn't have a mother?*

Pratap Singh looked at her and so did i. Both waiting for her to add on to what she just said. She wasn't even looking at me.

She took a step towards her father.

"We came to know the entire thing a couple of days back when we found her on top of the water tank. God knows what would have happened had we not found her on time!"

"You were not trying to take your life, were you?", asked Pratap Singh with a hint of rebuke in his voice.

I was too flabbergasted to say anything.

"Do you know it's a crime to commit suicide?".

How? I have always wondered, why do they term it as a crime when the person might already be dead before people can care! An unsuccessful attempt to kill yourself and then a lawsuit up your ass! What a way to make someone look forward to living a life!

But the man here was showing genuine concern and I didn't want to be the one ruining it. The story of my life was becoming increasingly interesting. She had a vivid imagination, and I wanted to hear where this was going!

"Don't be too hard on her baba! She has learnt from her mistake and she wants to start her life anew!"

"Of course she should! No one should decide for you have to do with your life apart from yourself. What are we without our freedom of choice!", the pitch of his voice getting higher with every word that appeared from behind his bushy moustache. Something I didn't know I had to get used to stay sane, at least at that point of time.

And freedom of choice! Ha! What an irony!

I just looked at Mallika who had just about managed to portray herself as a hero in front of her father, and a man, who probably was dumb, or deaf, or both! He had not as much as lifted his head since the time I had walked inside that room. And that was annoying me, for no apparent reason. All I could see was his back and his small pony tail tied neatly behind his head. My curiosity coupled with my annoyance was starting to get the better of me. I started leaning to my left to see if I could get a better angle. But then my eyes caught Mallika trying to get the measure of what I was trying to do. And i had no choice but to control myself. I stepped back as she gestured me to follow her, again! This time outside the room!

Pratap Singh gave me one of his, what I later came to realize his trade mark half chuckle—half smile which he would give to the recipients of his bona fide sympathies.

As I headed out of the room, i heard Pratap Singh call the other man in the room by his name.

"Arjun!"

I ambled across the corridor behind Mallika the Master, still wondering what Arjun looks like.

One of the maids showed me my room. It was on the ground floor next to the kitchen. Must have been the store room or something which they had made into a bedroom, perhaps for that extra servant!

Didn't matter much, because it was still bigger than my room in Kanpur! The room was quite a humble contrast to the glamour of the rest of the Bhavan. But nevertheless, it had a bed, it had a ceiling fan, had a small window next to the bed which over saw the lawn and it had a bathroom attached to it. A refreshing change from having to queue up every morning to take my bath in Kanpur! My own bathroom!

I dragged myself to bed; too tired from all that had happened in the last two days. Too exhausted from turning over a new page in my life! As I closed my eyes, I didn't know what the next day held for me, but I was confident, whatever it was, it would be good.

* * *

CHAPTER 13

Before long, Ranipur Society had become the center of a hot piece of news for entire Kanpur. The point was not that a young girl had taken off; it was that Surender ji's daughter had taken off. Quite surprisingly a lot of people didn't notice the co-incidence between me taking off and Harry and Mallika not being around. Of course, Mona did but she was too flabbergasted to point it out. In fact, think she might have figured she didn't want to put her hands in the beehive and tick off the queen, Mallika.

I was a little wary for the first few days that Baba might have complained to the police and that they might land up in Pratap Singh Bhavan any day. That did not happen. I was also was wary that someday I might just see my picture in the missing section of the paper too with a reward for my bounty hunter. That did not happen either. At that point of time, it just didn't matter to me. And the thought that no one bothered to look me up, just added to my indifference.

The next morning, my sleep was cut short by a thunderous knock on my door. Tired from the journey, I dragged my feet to the door to open it. No one was there. But I saw the entire house looking busy already. The servants were running around. Everyone was doing something, someone mopping the floor, someone running to the kitchen. Groggy, I thought it still looked a little dark. I looked at the watch; it was five in the morning.

Coming from a family that I did, I was used to waking up early and running errands for my mother. But it was nothing like this. The mornings were lazy and typical. Mishra ji's cows would moo whilst I would gather the coal. Dev would do his early morning stretches on the terrace. Baba would be sitting outside the house with the toothbrush in hand for half an hour and not brush at all.

But the staff in Pratap Singh Bhavan looked like they were on a mission. No one spoke to each other. They all looked like they were in some kind of symphony. No one needed to be told what was to be done; there was no screaming around, it was like watching a well-organized factory. Or had I been in the medieval ages, a slave house!

I stopped a genial looking old man to ask what this was about. Was It something special today?

He paused for a moment and said, "No it's just Wednesday! Baba is going to start the aarti in half an hour so you better go and get ready!"

"Who is Baba?" But Ramu Kaka (I guessed that might be his name) didn't wait around to answer that.

Few minutes later when I came out of the room, I saw the entire house gathered in one place in one corner of the living room. Someone was doing the *aarti*. I couldn't see who it was. I covered my head and stood behind all the people. The man was dressed in a dhoti. And that's all. He was bare chested as he was doing the pooja. His hair neatly tied behind his head. From that I inferred, it must be Baba and Baba must be Arjun, who i saw in the office last evening.

I saw Mallika standing right behind Arjun. Surprisingly, Pratap Singh was not there. Neither was Harry. There was an old lady and two children.

I was getting anxious to see Arjun's face now. It was well over twenty hours in the house already and I had no clue what he looked like. Soon my wish was granted as the aarti got over in the next few minutes.

As he turned around to pass on the thaali, I saw Arjun for the first time. He was a tall man, around six feet one, well built, his shoulders bulging out. His bristly chest looked strong and his hair neatly tied back. But there was something about his face. Strong jawed; he looked intimidating, and the eyes! The dark, broody eyes had such intensity in them, the kind that stares right through your soul and when he looked at me, he did! He kept his eyes on me for a moment and looked away. He showed no emotion.

Mallika invited me for breakfast and showed me my chair. It was right opposite hers and next to the children. She told me non-chalantly that is where I was expected to sit whenever I sat on the table. I found that weird. But then that was one of the hundred strange rules that existed in the house.

As I sat next to one of the children, she nudged me on my feet and asked me through her cute little spectacles. "Who are you?"

I whispered,. "I'm Bittu!"

She looked puzzled for a minute and the she asked me, "but who are you?"

I saw Mallika looking at me and I remembered her simple instruction. "Don't open your mouth!"

And so I didn't.

"I am Archana!", she said softly. I just smiled at her.

"I'm twelve, how old are you?"

93

"And who's that?" I asked about the other girl sitting next to her, the quite one.

"She is Rachna; she is younger to me, by 8 minutes!"

Mallika had two twelve year old daughters. I looked at her in amazement. She must have had them really young. Cause she looked quite young to be a mother of two kids. And Harry! He had a beautiful wife and two young daughters and that didn't stop him from being the scum he was!

The menu on the breakfast table gave me an insight as to why the servants had to wake up so early. The sheer variety of items satiated my appetite.

Pratap Singh joined us with his thunderous *Good Morning.* The morning almost felt good when he said that. He was dressed in his usual khaadi kurta which was neatly pressed. He gave me a big smile and the kids' even bigger kisses. The kids loved their grandpa. I didn't know much about him at that time but I could see why. He was a loud character and I had never met anyone in my life who could smile so constantly. He would wear that trademark smile almost as a generic expression.

Arjun came and sat next to Pratap Singh. One look at that breakfast table and you could figure out the dynamics of the family. I knew Arjun was family. But didn't exactly know where he fit in the picture. I didn't have to wait too long to get my answer though.

"We have a guest here!" he said. I couldn't quite understand it was a statement or a question. He was not even looking at me, something disdainful about his indifference. Or so I thought.

'Oh yes!', said Pratap Singh clapping his hand once.

"This is the young lady Mallika brought to our office last evening! You were there Arjun!".

"I wasn't paying attention!".

I felt offended. Why was he so grumpy!

"Well then! She is Bittu!" he said pointing towards me.

'And Bittu, that's my son, Arjun Pratap Singh!' pride gleaming in his eyes.

Arjun Pratap Singh.

Now that's a name, I said to myself. I almost felt embarrassed about my name there. My growing consciousness about it off late was making it worse for me than it was.

And then he asked the question that I dreaded being asked, "So why are you here?". I didn't realise that question was directed towards me. Until I looked up from my plate and realized he was waiting for me to answer that.

He was looking straight at me, almost as if he could smell something was cooking. That looked unnerved me.

I looked at Mallika who was sitting on the left of Pratap Singh.

"Well, she is going to be with us from now!" said Mallika.

He didn't show any emotion. He didn't ask anything after that. Almost as if it didn't matter to him!

Arjun Pratap Singh was a walking genetic paradox to his father. If Pratap Singh was loud and boisterous, Arjun Pratap Singh was soft spoken. Almost as if he was whispering! If Pratap Singh had a word for every second of his living life, Arjun Pratap Singh was the most laconic man I had ever met in my life. He is the kinds that can survive on a lonely island without talking to his Man Friday! If Pratap Singh was never tired of wearing that smile on his face, it seemed to me Arjun Pratap Singh smiled on special occasions, like birthdays and Diwali!

But despite the picture that he painted, Arjun Pratap Singh was nothing like anyone I had ever met. His striking good looks were overshadowed by the sternness of his face. And to be honest I was scared of him. He was not creepy, he was scary!

"Baba I was thinking about Bittu last night and it just occurred to me, we should take her to *Asha*".

Asha? Who is that now, I thought!

"You spoke my mind Mallika, what better for her at this point of her life than Asha!", he said.

I was getting curious but I couldn't dare interrupt the conversation.

"We need to help her get back on her feet!" she said sounding almost sympathetic. Had I not known the agenda behind her interest in me, I would have actually believed her concern. Like Pratap Singh did!

"Yes we do! Take her today itself, introduce her and see if we can find something to keep her occupied with!"

I didn't know what to expect, so put my head down and started eating! Mallika was too full of surprises for my comfort, I was just glad she didn't murder me on our way to Mumbai. So I knew she wouldn't do anything to harm me at the moment.

I had but no choice to wait and find out what was in store for me!

*   *   *

CHAPTER 14

An hour later I was in the backseat of the car again! Mallika sat on the seat next to Arjun, who was driving the car!

"Are you going to tell me the real story now?" asked Arjun to Mallika as we stopped at a signal.

"You know the story!" said Mallika, completely stoic.

"You do realise there is bluff written all *over your face!' said* Arjun with a sarcastic smile.

Mallika didn't react to that. Arjun kept looking at her for a minute, realised he was not going to get anything more out of her. He just shook his head and kept driving.

We finally reached wherever we were supposed to be a few minutes later. I got my first taste of Mumbai's humidity that morning as I stepped out of the car. Perspiring profusely, I wondered what summers might be like there, which was still officially a month away. The sun was beating down at ten in the morning in its full glory. There was a thick smog just above which seemed to be forming a second atmosphere just atop Mumbai.

Mallika gestured me to follow her. Arjun stayed put in the car. As I followed Mallika, I realised that the place was a far cry from the posh locality where Pratap Singh Bhavan stood tall and proud.

We went past a few brick houses, which looked like encroachments. Anyone who passed by Mallika gave her a respectful *salaam*, the kids called her *taai* and she stroked their head playfully with lots of affection. She smiled at everyone as she was greeted with folded hands by these people, their faces that of utter gratitude.

We crossed a few of these houses and then we stood in front of a two storied building, immaculately painted and standing out like a well-bred horse in the stud farm of poorly constructed houses.

And as I stood in front of that house, I knew who Asha was!

Rather what Asha was!

Asha: A Second Chance at Life was plastered on a ten by eight hoarding as it hung from the second floor of the building.

It didn't take me long to assume that this was an equivalent of an orphanage or old age house. And that I would be disposed off here before long like an extra piece of baggage in the name of charity!

"Come inside!", said Mallika. I followed her.

As we stepped inside, I started getting an idea what the place was about. Seated on the front desk which looked like a reception was a short portly woman who must have been in her fifties!

"Mallika *madam, tumhi itni sakali sakali",* I had no clue what she said, my knowledge of Marathi was just a zilch! The old woman had immediately stood up, albeit with a bit of difficulty as I saw, when Mallika walked in. I was certain Mallika was someone important to this place.

"Aaji, tumhi basa! Yeh Bittu hai, mere pehchan ki hai. Kisi se kehke isko Asha dikha do. Aur ek baat, iske liye yahaan pe koi kaam dhoondo! (Aaji, you sit! This is Bittu, my acquaintance. Ask someone to show her around the place. And one more thing, find some work for her here!).

The last bit did not in the least bit surprise me. I was certain I didn't just want to sit around in the house. I was certain I already bid good bye to any further scope of education. So might as well do something that would keep me occupied. I was also conscious at the same time about pursuing my dreams about singing. My innocence was convinced that by some divine intervention the doors of opportunities would open up for me and I would walk right through it into the arms of my destiny. But somewhere deep in my heart I was aware that my life had taken a turn even I would have found hard to explain; that it would take nothing less than a miracle to keep my dreams alive.

As I followed the elderly woman around, who I noticed was walking with a slight limp inclined towards her left, I looked around the building. The place was as bright on the inside as it was outside. It was well-ventilated and the bright light of mid-morning sunshine was gushing through the wooden windows. I noticed that Mallika was walking close to our heels.

"Bittu, you said your name was, correct?" asked the old woman finally breaking the silence between us.

I nodded in affirmation.

"What's yours?" I asked in Hindi, addressing her with the customary *aap*.

"My name is Laxmi! However, you can call me *Aaji* as everyone prefers to call me here!" she said with a cheerful grin on her face. Though I didn't know what Aaji meant, I was certain it was the Marathi equivalent of addressing someone senior with as much respect as fondness.

"What do you know about Asha?", she asked in brisk Marathi. Of course, I didn't understand a word except for the fact that she had asked me a question, by the tone of her voice.

"Tujhe marathi nahin aati ya bolna nahin aata?", she asked with another cheerful grin after a min when she realised I haven't answered. This she asked in Hindi. I was hardly offended by that, her face suggested that she this was her usual playful demeanour.

"*Ji,* I don't speak Marathi. I just came to Mumbai!", I said meekly.

"So you do speak!", she said with another laugh, "good for you, good for you!".

"Anyways, I asked do you know anything about Asha?" she asked, this time her tone a little less playful I noticed.

I said no.

"Well, then listen! Asha was founded in 1975 by our beloved Asha Rani Singh, when she was hardly 24 years of age. Oh what a spritely young soul she was! And beautiful!" she exclaimed.

And as if she read my mind which had only one question at that time, who was Asha Rani Singh?

"*Asha ji* was Mallika's mother." The mention of her name and I looked around reflexively. But she was not there, I wondered where she went.

"How did she come about with Asha?"

"Well that's a long story! I will have to sit down for that and I hope you have time for that".

Of course I had the time, what other business had I to attend to?

I just smiled and confirmed by affirmation.

"The late sixties and 70's were a time of change, parivartan; in the political flavour I mean. Especially our brothers and sisters in the eastern part of the country, particularly in Bengal were slowly fathoming a storm."

"A storm?" I asked.

"Yes a storm", she said with a glint in her eyes as if she had transcended the boundaries of time and landed right in the era and the place.

"Naxalism was picking up! The country was on the brink of war with Pakistan! Still reeling from the Indio-Chini war! The Government was tracking down young students, college going students at that and making mass arrests! There were talks about conspiracy in the dark alleys and hush in the *gallis*. The roads were red with the blood of our youth. Bombay, long before it was Mumbai, was still the dream capital of our country. It was a safe haven, at least for the lives if not for the dreams." I noticed the rueful inflection at that last sentence.

"Tonnes of people were moving out of different cities and flocking the streets of Bombay, some in search of a new chapter in their lives, some with dreams as big as becoming a cinema star and some because they didn't belong anywhere!"

"What do you mean by they didn't belong anywhere?", I asked.

"Have you not heard of refugees beta! They are, as they saying goes, *the disinherited beings who belong neither to the past nor the future"* And to this day that saying remains carved in my memory.

"Was Asha Rani Singh a refugee?" I asked curiously.

This invited a loud laughter from her. "Don't say that aloud my dear! Mallika is very sensitive with her lineage! She would not take that kindly!" I could only imagine.

"To tell you the truth, she belonged to a pretty well-off family of advocates and magistrates and bureaucrats in Calcutta! Her grandfather was a well-known Leftist in those days! Her mother was a judge of good repute and father was typical bureaucrat with lots of contact with the inner circles of who's who of the political world." I was intrigued by Aaji's crisp choice of words as she narrated the tale. I would hardly have expected to hear things such as Leftist and Naxals and talks about the bureaucrats from a woman like her. Her personality hardly fit the words she was saying.

"Her name doesn't sound like a Bengali name?" I asked curiously.

"Yes indeed! She was of Bengali origin and her maiden name was Asha Rani. She never used her father's last name which was Chatterjee!"

"Why is that?"

"Asha was always somewhat of what you call as rebel! She didn't find it obligatory to flaunt her father's lineage through her name. Instead she chose to use her mother's name as her last name!"

"Well then how come she ended up taking the last name Singh?" And as I said that I figured the old frail women I had seen in the morning was her.

"When women love, they love with everything!" She said with a smile, "Even with their names!"

Aaji had a nostalgic wrinkle on her forehead which suggested that she has lived this story in her head many a times. She paused for a moment and then turned around hastily.

"Anyways, enough information for first day! Rest of it, some other day, I have some business to attend to!"

To this day I hate incomplete stories, and hated it then too! Aaji had given a theatrical opening to the story, I was just getting interested and she had cut short. But my mind had carelessly wandered off to the old woman I had seen in the morning. I wondered how she had become so quiet and almost ghostly.

I followed Aaji, mostly because I didn't have anything to do. I couldn't find Mallika anywhere. I was relieved though that she was not around. I could breathe!

* * *

CHAPTER 15

It had been two weeks since and the *gallis* of Ranipur Society were still abuzz with the gossip of me having taken off. Baba had gone about with his daily routines, pretending nothing had happened. He would simply walk past any jibes made at him or even the sympathetic look of our neighbors who would ask him if he had any news about me. Baba always had this defense mechanism where he would just go about his life without letting anything affect him. Almost robotic! But it was my brother Dev who was shaken up the most. As the days passed and they didn't hear anything from me, his anger had given way to worry. Of course, there were the usual cheap talks he had to hear about me from his friends and all, about me being a whore and having walked out with a pimp.

It was not long before people had started adding up two and two as my leaving town had strangely co-incided with Mallika and Harry leaving without a notice. Dimpy and Mona had no doubt what so ever that something had transpired overnight and that Mallika had a doing in whatever happened. However, they didn't dare spell out anything, such was Mallika's terror! As far as I was concerned, I was still far away from sparing a thought about all this. I had paid no attention to anything remotely connected to Ranipur Society from the moment I stepped away from it.

I had started helping Aaji at Asha. I was given the responsibility of teaching a small classroom of around 20 women, who were aged anything between 5 and 35. Most of these women stayed at Asha, however, some even were from the nearby basti. I had started enjoying teaching this group as there was something really interesting about them. Despite their limited means of livelihood, they had all this amazing sense of self respect, which spawned out of the fact that they were independent, strong women and bread winners. These women were not women of letter but they had no dearth of dignity. I was their teacher, yet I was the one learning.

Aaji was an absolutely wonderful influence on everyone around her. She was constantly passing on some learning about life through one of her numerous own experiences. There was almost motherly warmth in the way she held all of us close to her. It was not difficult to understand why she was revered by all. Aaji was the unsung hero behind the success of Asha, she was the backbone of this family. Asha Rani trusted her blindly, so they said. Two weeks and I had not seen her once yet there. So much so for founding it, I thought! But the curiosity to know about her was tugging away at me. Everyday as I travelled in the locals back home from Sion to Bandra, holding thinly on to the last breath of my life trying not to be caught up in merry stampede, I would think about the old frail face I would see only once a day, during the morning Puja at home. I had never heard her speaking and I was convinced that she was suffering from some kind of terminal disease. I never heard anyone at the house speaking to her either, at least to my knowledge.

The other character in this house that really intrigued me was Arjun. He was extremely polite to everyone and his general tone when he spoke was that of respect towards the other person, a trait rare for a man of his means. He never missed performing the morning aarti and there was an aura about him in his bare-chested dhoti clad look. He was intimidating and his careful choice of words; his general laconic being used to make me nervous. He was aware of that and that made me more nervous. He had long hair and I had never seen them untied from his ponytail. I saw very less of him during the weekdays. But as time passed and Pratap Singh had started insisting that I spend more time at home at least during the weekends, which he insisted of others too, I gradually started to see him more. He had this strange look whenever he saw me; a look that suggested that he knew I was Mallika's bitch. To be fair to be him, I had become one. Mallika was such a powerful presence to be around that it was impossible to say no to anything that she asked of me. Be it from teaching at Asha to fetch her clothes from the dry cleaners. She insisted that if I wanted to be a part of the house, I needed to the chores, which I didn't mind. I didn't earn much at Asha but my expenses were virtually next to nil. I would have my meals at home, I had something that something most people in my situation in a city like Mumbai would kill to have; a place to sleep, rent free!

It didn't take me much time to settle down in Pratap Singh Bhavan though. My interactions with the family members had become more casual. Pratap Singh had taken a liking to my simplicity, he would say. He would say that at least twice a day, to which Harry always had a sarcastic grin. He had started introducing me to his inner circle of trusted allies and friends as another trusted member. He insisted that I be a part of some of the less controversial party discussions. Sunday evenings were mostly reserved for this and I had started looking forward to these gatherings. Initially, all I could hear was either the extremities of high pitched arguments suggesting discord or the intention hush—hush of coarse voices suggesting whatever the topic was, was meant to be within the confines of the four walls.

Mallika never had any problems with Pratap Singh making me a part of all this, at least she never made it clear. However, Arjun was never comfortable speaking in front of me. He couldn't fathom what a 17 year old was anyways supposed to be learning from all this. In any case, I knew that although he was not going out of his way to find out about me, but he didn't beleive Mallika's version of the story. As a result, his general attitude towards me was that of curious doubt. I was always conscious of being alone with him anywhere, be it in an elevator, on the dinner table or if were just walking out of the house together. I knew that one day he would either find out and confront me, or just confront me to find out. But knowing that he had great respect for Mallika would soothe my nerves. Then again, his love for Pratap Singh was beyond question. Three months and I knew that if you didn't mean well for Pratap Singh, Arjun Singh would teach you to do so!

Not once had I seen him with it but I knew he had a gun. Probably that was what scared me most about him. He had never come home with bruises or bleeding across his face. But one had to see his entourage to know what I am saying. He had two sidekicks, who were typically muscularly built who had nothing remotely civilized going about them or so I thought. Both were brutes who would force a smile everytime they would meet Pratap Singh, and when they did show their toothy grin, one would wonder what's all the fuss about a smile! They looked like two trained wild beasts flanking Arjun Singh from right and left. And it was in their being so tame around him that would establish Arjun's unrelenting authority.

Nevertheless, life was moving at a fairly brisk pace, much faster than how it was in Kanpur. A day to a month, a month to three, three to six and before long it was a year since I had left Kanpur! Asha had become a part of my life, it had started defining me. It was slowly opening me up to a different side of me where I was happy living trying to make someone else's life better. But then there are things you cant keep down for too long. In my case, it was what brought me to Mumbai!

CHAPTER 16

"What's all that noise about?" i asked one of the maids at home as I heard what sounded like a one sided argument behind a closed door.

"Mallika madam ji!", was all she said.

The suppressed voice was coming from the bedroom beyond the stairs which I knew to be the one that was always closed. It was Asha Rani's room. I had never heard the sound of even a pin drop from that room. It was the first time in a year I had heard a voice from the room. I was curious. I tried to listen as I strained my ears, walking slowly up the stairs. I was curious if it was Asha Rani talking so animatedly. I had never heard her speak. I didn't know what she sounded like. She was just a face to me, that didn't speak! The room was like a closed dungeon in one corner of the house. Only Mallika was allowed to go in, thrice a day, twice with food and once with her medicines. The only time Asha Rani would be seen out of her room was in the morning during the daily aarti. She was like a ghost, no one acknowledged her presence. She was like the walls in the house, who we saw everyday but didn't feel it necessary to hug or talk to!

I climbed the flight of stairs and turned towards the right, tip toeing like a cat, careful not to be found out. I stopped right outside the door which was almost shut, open enough to allow a string of light to pass through. Or the voice to perforate across the room!

"Years of my life I have lived in shame and hiding because of you! Not being able to acknowledge who I m, living a life of lie! And you stand here, staring at me every day with your blank eyes!" the voice was teethed, yet I knew that was Mallika's.

"The tables have turned, haven't they? I am not willing to let it go! I have earned where I stand."

I didn't have the slightest idea what the conversation was about, yet I knew there was more to Pratap Singh Bhavan than met the eye. The high and mighty walls of this house held secrets that were locked behind closed doors. Maybe the eyes of those who lived here saw what was to be seen but have chosen to ignore them. I knew I had become part of something complex and didn't want to be. But as I walked away from there, I realised one more thing, I had to know what Mallika was upto. I needed to know one of her secrets to leverage against mine!

For the next few days I just slyly observed Mallicka. Or so I tried! The fact that everything in the house was so discrete made it impossible for me to find out what was happening. I hardly spent much time inside the house. Most of my time was spent at Asha. I however intended to spy around as much as possible whenever I was home. But it was not working. Mallicka never chose a specific time to go inside the room. She somehow managed to slip in quietly. The fact that none of the other family members ever asked about Asha Rani probably made it a lot easier for her to hide whatever she was hiding.

She followed a particular pattern to make sure everyone had something to do just about the time she was about to go to Asha Rani's room. The maids for example, were sent off to buy something or the other, or to clean the already impeccably cleaned garden all over again, or Arjun to collect some money from someone or to finish some unfinished business. It was always something or the other. With me she never bothered much, as I hardly ever dared to poke my nose around in her business. And though I was not, I was comfortable with the idea that she thought I was afraid of her.

*   *   *

115

"Where you off to so late in the night?" inquired Mallika one late summer night as Arjun was about to leave the house, in a bit of high spirits to be honest. He had what looked like an attempt of a smile on his face.

"Well, I told you I have to go to the airport, the flight lands in twenty minutes!".

"Should I wait up?", asked Mallika. Arjun was probably the only person she showed a little concern for. For all others it looked as if she was doing everything more out of duty than anything else.

"Never mind, by the time we come back its going to be two in the morning! Will meet at breakfast tomorrow!"

"Or maybe lunch", Mallika smiled, waived and walked off up the stairs.

I was right there but neither seemed to notice me. As if I had blended into the background. But that was hardly on my mind that time! I wondered who was coming! Until ten minutes back, I didn't know that Pratap Singh Bhavan was expecting a guest. There was no apparent preparatory signs! But then there never was, unlike my house in Kanpur, where we had to plan for at least week if someone was visiting us. Where would the guest sleep, the mattresses would go for a mandatory cleaning and drying on the terrace; what would the guests eat, different sorts of food items would be stored up. All just to play a good host! And for most of the times for people I didn't give a fuck for! Baba's unreasonable demand to parade me in front of the guests, trying to showcase my singing talents had gotten to my nerves in the last few years! One of his old school mates had a taste of it, when I "accidentally" dropped the piping hot cup of tea on his shirt the moment he asked me to sing! Fuck off, I thought!

But nothing in this house was remotely close to Kanpur! There was a guest expected at the house and no one showed any emotion about it. If Arjun was going to pick whoever this person was, he had to be someone of importance. Was he an old family friend of the Singhs, was he one of Arjun's college friends or was he a political alliance of Pratap Singh? Too many questions, i didn't have the answer to any!

I went to bed comfortable with the idea that I was going to meet him at the breakfast table next morning! I had a day off from Asha the next day, the first in months; I wished to sleep till late into the morning!

* * *

My head was spinning the next morning as I drowsily came to the realization that someone was banging at the door. I looked at the wall clock hanging straight in front of my bed! It was ten o'clock. My jaws almost dropped. Sleeping till ten in Pratap Singh Bhavan was almost a crime!

117

Unless you were dead, you were supposed to be outside your rooms by eight thirty at the latest. Also, the urgency of the knock on the door suggested there was something important to attend to! I was afraid it was Mallika. And as I walked towards the door, I prepared myself for an early morning rebuke from her. But it was not her. It was her daughter—Rachna.

"Come for breakfast Bittu didi!" she said in an urgent voice and started running off, looking visibly excited.

I called after her to understand the situation. But she didn't seem to take note. She was clearly just sent to summon me.

Then as the sleep subsided from my dreary eyes a bit I realised the guest must also be at the table. I quickly went to the bathroom, that's where I had a mirror, to see how horrible I looked! I was not a morning person! But then it would be difficult to pick any time of the day when it came to me. I tied up my hair, in the last year if anything had started looking better, it was my hair! It had grown considerably. Since I didn't oil it every day now, it had gotten a bit of texture as well. I put on a t shirt and a slacks and I went to the breakfast table.

"Good Morning!", said a loud and cheerful voice. *That of a girl. And it was not Mallika.* For a minute, I didn't realise which part of the dining table I should be looking at. And then as my eyes traced

Arjun, my eyes fell on her sitting next to him. With a huge grin on her face!

*   *   *

As it turns out, the guest expected at Pratap Singh Bhavan was not a *he!* Long, curly hairs flowing down her shoulder untidily, kissing her neck, a few strands reaching to her face, a few longing to touch her forehead; clearly indicating she was just out of bed and a bit weary from the travel. She wore a loose white t shirt that had "I LOVE NY" printed in bold red, and a pair of tights that reached till her ankle. She sat on the side of the table that was close to the window of the dining room. The morning sun was shining on her bouncy hair. It looked as if she standing in a spotlight. It would have fit to say I had never come across a prettier woman in my life. And surprisingly enough, it didn't make me conscious this time.

"Have a seat Bittu!", she said with a big smile.

How the hell does she know my name, I thought and who the hell are you anyways?

I sat down with an apparently quizzical look on my face. Arjun seemed to notice that. Pratap Singh was not at the table that morning. He had gone to attend an election rally. I was surprised that Arjun and Mallika had not gone with them. It was a first for me!

119

"She is Mugdha!", said Arjun. He kept quiet after that, as if that made all the sense to me! I kept on looking at him until he realized. Mugdha in the meanwhile was just looking at us and smiling. Why is she so happy, I thought!

"She is a *very* close friend of mine!" I noticed the stress on *very* although I doubt it was intentional. He was not one to hint at anything to make it obvious. Though it didn't take a scientist to understand that they were more than friends!

Everyone at the table seemed pretty comfortable with her, including Mallika's daughters. It was obvious she was a familiar face in the family although I had never being spoken about since the time I was staying at Pratap Singh Bhavan.

I did not say much at the table. I never had much to say anyways but I kept shy of the usual small talks as well. My life in Asha was a diametrically opposite to what I had expected to do in Mumbai. There was no glamour, no spotlight, no recognition. Yet Asha was starting to give me a sense of freedom. It was the taste of something new for me. I was starting to enjoy it.

My equation with Mallika was comfortable. Though she refrained from discussing personal matters with me at length, there were times when she would talk in front of me to her father or brother and didn't seem to mind my presence. Even at Asha, she was giving me responsibilities that generally took anyone else two to three years to earn. Aaji was particularly impressed by my politeness and always put in a kind word for me. She was a real shrewd woman though.

She was certain that there was more to my story than I had disclosed. She would often ask about my parents at different times to see if my version of truth differed any time. But I stuck to Mallika's version of running away/being rescued as I didn't want to be married off early. I did have the advantage of looking a bit vulnerable with my kajal-less eyes, and faint smile. Initially whoever heard my story sympathized with me. The strange thing is the more I narrated the story, the more I believed in it.

Aaji made me share my story with the women at Asha. She thought it would be of inspiration to them. That women need to stand up for their own rights! Soon as the original story had started losing its sheen, I had started adding more details to it. Like how I was kept locked in a room once without food for two days, how I revolted against my father when he was discussing dowry with one of the suitors. Little details, however, over a period of time had made my story really interesting.

I was few months over eighteen now and I was asked to give an interview for a local newspaper. I was conscious that it shouldn't print in Kanpur but I was assured it would be only printed in the City section of a Marathi paper.

Mallika did not seem to mind the modified story. She never confronted me as to why I was cooking it all up and to this extent. She knew what it felt to be at the center of people's attention and she was letting me be in it. She had her own reasons for it too. Every time my story of apparent mental torture was narrated, inevitably it would lead to Mallika and her heroics of saving me.

At the end of the year, I was the young, bold social worker who was touching the lives of many women across the city. One newspaper described me as the *"innocent nightingale who escaped the cage of fear and male domination and now healing a thousand women through her mellifluous voice and therapeutic singing"* while Mallika was the *hero every society needed*!

Pratap Singh too benefitted from the entire mirage of reality. Of course, he believed what we told him. Somewhere I was always worried he would come to know eventually, his network of sycophants stretched far and wide. He had unquestionable trust on Mallika. That made it a lot easier than it should have been. His election campaigns too got a boost from being the mascot of the family. He had reservations about exploiting my story for his political gains as the kind man he was, he didn't want to invade my privacy. But I let him and Mallika let him on the pretext that on the contrary, it was emboldening women to speak up across the city. Something he could relate to more closely.

Harry was a mute spectator to all that was happening. He did not say much, not that it would have mattered. No one seemed to pay any attention to him. He was more like the errand boy of the house who happened to enjoy a slightly higher status than the rest of the servants. He mostly stayed away from the house. Arjun was not too fond of him. He was pretty vocal about it. He wouldn't leave any chance to take jibes at his worthlessness.

Despite all this, what surprised me was how a woman like Mallika was married to a man like that in the first place. There was probably more to the story than I knew. There was no way it was out of love, if it was, then love is indeed blind. Or Mallika was! The only explanation I could think was that this was some sort of arrangement that had resulted from a political agreement. I didn't know much about Harry's background so that theory also ran into a wall. Though I never felt too inclined to know the actual story, I was also wary of broaching the subject with anyone in the house.

Arjun's general attitude over the year had not changed much which was border line indifference however there were times when he would just quietly smile at us with a look that suggested he couldn't be fooled. I was quite certain he didn't know the entire truth about the situation which landed me in Mumbai. But the story that we had presented was a hoax. He of course never questioned Mallika, or at least in front of me. There was also the part where I knew if Arjun knew what Harry had done, he would have shot him, at least once in the leg if not at his head. The fact that he was still alive assured me he didn't know much. He like his father had unquestionable trust in Mallika. It almost pained me sometimes to see how two men of such great character and intelligence allowed themselves to be fooled by Mallika. Maybe it was that as a family they were very close and nothing took that away. But then again, who was I to question Mallika's ways. I was remorseless about how I painted my family in front of the world.

*   *   *

CHAPTER 17

Once breakfast was over, I went to the kitchen to see everything was in place. I was learning a bit of cooking from the old cook of the house—Nasim. He was a kind hearted man in his late sixties and had been working in Pratap Singh Bhavan for more than thirty years. That meant he was privy to a lot of information about the house but like everyone else under that roof, his loyalty was unflinching. When it came to matters of the house, he too like the others was a wall. There but almost inanimate. Witnessing but never giving out!

"Yours' is quite a story!" I didn't realise Mugdha was standing behind me.

"I am sorry?" I turned around to face her. She had an apple in her hand and was wearing an effervescent smile. *Damn she is beautiful*, I thought.

"Arjun told me about your story! Sorry if I am prying!" she said the smile still on her face. It was almost as if that was her natural expression.

"That's ok. People seem to take keen interest in sorry stories!" I said. It must have sounded a bit curt although I didn't intend to.

"I wouldn't put it that way! People like to be inspired! You are someone a lot of women relate to in this part of the world!"

"Speaking of which, where are you from? Arjun never mentioned anything about you until this morning. That was not much detail".

"Ah you know him. Always a private person", she said waving her hand, taking another bite of the apple. I noticed she was not wearing any lip stick but her lips were pink enough. Men must find her irresistible.

"Too private for comfort sometimes! Never says much but seems to know every detail of other's life!" I meant it.

"You don't seem to like him!" she arrived at the conclusion.

"Well I wouldn't put it that way, I don't dislike him, but I am not sure I like him either", I said with a smile.

"You are not the only one with that opinion. He has always been like this, doesn't open up much. I have known him for close to twenty years, since we were a child. There are parts of his life, even I am not sure of."

"Why is that? I take it you are close to this family?"

"I am! My mother dated Arjun's dad for some time until she had a change of heart and married his best friend", she said as a matter of fact. That caught my attention.

"You mean you are Desai *saab's* daughter!"

"Yes! They managed to overlook the entire fiasco and have remained friends all these years; which meant I was always around here till I was sixteen! I have practically grown up in this house. Arjun and I are almost of the same age."

"So where did you go after you turned sixteen?"

"Well, I always wanted to see the world, never can stay at one place for too long. So I decided to move to New York to study further". She was now sitting on the kitchen slab next to the oven. Nasim chacha had left the kitchen to let us continue with our talks.

"It was a question of just you deciding?" I didn't know the world functioned this way. All I wanted was to go to Mumbai. I felt inclined to ask her who she had to sleep with for that. I didn't!

"Yes of course, it's my life. It had to be my decision at the end of the day. It does matter a lot that money wasn't a factor for me, dad has plenty!" she said with a giggle.

Her laughter was almost childlike, infectious.

"You of all people should know what it's like to take your own decision", she continued.

"Trust me; I have a lot of respect for you! It takes a lot to stand up like the way you did!" I was embarrassed.

"You and I are going to be friends, aren't we?" she said as she hopped on to the floor from the foot high kitchen slab.

I smiled back at her. She walked out of the kitchen, the smell of her shampoo still lingering.

I liked her. We could be friends, I thought.

"Don't corrupt her!" said Arjun through the little window in the kitchen that was facing the lawn. He had been watering the plants.

Before I could react, he had turned his face and had walked away. Typical! But this somehow enraged me! I was getting tired of his laconic jibes.

I marched out to the lawn. I saw him bathing the dogs in the lawn. Mugdha was not there.

"What do you mean?" he looked at me and without the slightest change in expression looked away.

I was furious now.

"I asked you something!", I almost screamed.

"At that pitch, it's hard to miss what you are saying, even if I wanted to!"

"Oh a full sentence! So you are not demented after all!" I couldn't believe I said that.

He looked at me in surprise. And then he just allowed himself a smile.

"What the hell are you laughing at?" I was walking towards him.

He ignored. I was in no mood to let him off today.

I went and grabbed the water pipe he was using to bathe his dog. He grabbed at it, I pulled it. He was a strong man, he didn't seem to budge. I gave it a harder pull, and all of a sudden he released his grip. I fell back with the recoil. The water pouring on me! That seemed to have amused him. He let out a loud laughter. For the first time in my life I saw him laughing.

He saw that I was refusing to get back, seething in anger!

He pulled himself together and offered a hand for me to get up.

"I still want to know what you meant by what you said?", I asked as I grabbed on to his hand and stood back on my feet again. I was almost wet.

"You know what I mean Bittu!" he said, his tone today a lot less serious than I had ever heard.

"No I don't!"

"Well then let me spell it out for you!" I was curious to know what he had to say.

"You think everyone in this whole wide world is a damned fool. You have been strutting around in my house for the last year as if you belong here. I don't know what have you been scheming with my sister. Not because I can't find out but because I have respected whatever decision Mallika has taken. But Mugdha is different. She doesn't understand the politics of life. So I'm saying the day I find out that you are so much so as trying to corrupt Mugdha, I will take your mask off. I know you are neither a victim nor a hero! You are just an opportunist! So don't pretend in front of me!"

He said all of that in one breathe. For the first time Arjun had spoken with me openly and he had stripped me of my lie. I stood there feeling bare in front of him not knowing whether to confront him, contradict him or slap him!

I waited for a minute as he kept on staring at him. I turned around and started walking away.

"Loser!" I heard him say.

* * *

That night well past mid night I came out of my room to drink some water. I was walking to the kitchen when a sudden intuition dragged me up the stairs and towards the second room towards the right—in the direction of Arjun's room. I could see there was faint light seeping underneath the door, maybe the night lamp. I thought I heard something fall inside the room. I pressed my ear up against the door and I heard heavy breathing in the dead of the night. I was curious. I probably knew what was going on but I still wanted to know. I knelt down and put my eye on the key hole of the door. My heart racing fast! Had anyone seen me there I would have been dead meat. But my curiosity got the better of me. The breathing got heavier. I strained my eyes as the light from the night lamp did not make the vision any clearer. The long curly hair, the well-built chest, the infectious smile and the ponytail seemed all too familiar. Their bodies intertwined as they were making love on the Arjun's study table. Her legs wrapped around her waist, his head buried in her neck. I wanted to go away couldn't for at least two minutes. Finally, I thought I saw Mugdha staring at the key hole of the door. It made me nervous. As I walked away I was certain she couldn't have known I was there. It was pitch dark and I didn't make any sound.

My first experience at voyeurism, I thought as I walked away quietly into my room.

*　　*　　*

Next morning I was in the kitchen again when Mugdha came prancing with the apple in her hand. All vibrant and happy! Arjun was a little relaxed too at the breakfast table. They seemed to have had a good night.

She just stood watching me do my chores. I was waiting for her to speak but she kept on chewing the apple. Finally I broke the silence.

"More than friends' right?" I said rhetorically.

"So you watched the show, right?" she answered with a question. She burst out laughing after that.

"How did you know?" I was going red.

"Well I wasn't sure who was outside the room but you made sure you answer my doubts by asking me!"

"Stupid me!" I tapped my head. "I am sorry, I didn't mean to pry!"

"Of course you did!' she said "But that's ok! Just make sure you don't do that again, kind of creepy to be honest!"

Despite the weirdness of the conversation, I was not feeling that uncomfortable. Such was her effect. I could see why Arjun was so relaxed after she had come to the house. I wondered what if Arjun had seen me. He would have stared me into oblivion.

"To answer your question, we are definitely more than friends. Strange you don't know, you have been here for more than a year now!"

I shook my head, I didn't know!

"But we haven't been able to define it yet. I was in fact engaged to him a few years back but that was more out of my father and his father wanting us to settle down than anything else."

"Engaged? What happened then?"

"Well I moved back to New York, kind of cheated on him!"

"You don't seem to be the types!", I said.

"Well there is a fine line. He had told me he had started liking someone else; I didn't take it too well! I might have even started falling in love with him so it hurt me a bit. Of course, the gentleman he is, he told me before he told the woman he liked so there was nothing between them. But I got wasted that night, and slept with a total stranger! The typical bar—drunk—morning of repentance story!"

I didn't know what was typical about that but I figured in her part of the world it was chronic!

"So?"

"I told him the truth and broke up with him. He didn't want to call it off because he did not want me to be the villain of this story! He is a wonderful guy!"

"So what did you tell your parents?"

"He took the blame, he said he didn't want to get married, wanted to focus on the party and whatever he does! He got into a major fight with his father, he almost threw him out but he didn't utter a word! Finally, I and my father had to talk sense into Pratap uncle's head."

"Wow! I didn't know he had a life!" I was thinking out aloud.

"Of course he has! There are few like him, he just doesn't want people to know this side of his!"

"He doesn't necessarily have to carry a gun!"

Her eyebrows immediately came together.

"What the fuck? He carries a gun?" she screamed. She didn't seem to know that part.

"You didn't know?" I said; shocked knowing my doom was near.

"Of course I didn't! Why?"

"How do I know why? But promise me you won't tell him I spurted this out. Else my head will be hanging as a show piece on the wall outside!"

She nodded. She looked a little worried. She kept quiet for a minute.

"If you guys are not together, he likes someone else, what was all that last night?"

"That's physical, plus we are comfortable with each other. As far as the other girl is concerned, she is not in the picture anymore but that's not my story to tell. If you find the courage, ask him", the smile back on her face. She knew I wasn't going to be able to gather enough strength in a lifetime to do that.

Arjun identified me as an opportunist. He knew that I was milking the situation. He still chose to ignore it. Too many questions had started queuing up in my mind. Why wasn't he interested to find out the true story, was he not concerned about the well-being of his father, I could have been a bomb strapping assassin, after all he was a known political figure. What happened to the women Mugdha was talking about? Despite all these doubts I was certain that Arjun knew how to be in control without letting anyone know. He was clearly doing some dirty work for his father and sister. He was not a mafia but I couldn't put a finger to it what was his role in the entire scheme of things. He was not Pratap Singh's assistant, he didn't interfere much in decisions, and he was more of the person who was responsible for execution.

For days as we ran into each other, I had the quizzical look on my face. He knew something was on my mind and that I might ask him a few questions. But the look and the smile on his face suggested he was sure, I didn't have the courage or yet, to ask anything.

I was not sure what Mugdha's purpose of visit was. She was always around, happy and chirpy, a bit nosy sometimes. But no one seemed to mind that. Mallika too was visibly fond of her. I hadn't got any further opportunity to find out what was the story behind Asha Rani as well. But I was certain Mugdha had an idea about it. It was a matter of patience when would she broach the subject! She was a chatty girl and she needed someone to talk to all the time. After the first few days had passed and Arjun had become engrossed in his usual busy hours, Mugdha had long hours of doing nothing. Just at home! I was certain her inquisitive attitude would help me dig up something.

* * *

CHAPTER 18

"You stupid, stupid fool!" screamed Mugdha once I was done with my music class at Asha. Mugdha had started frequenting Asha but this was the first time she had found time to sit through the music class where I tutored the little girls.

We had not left the class yet so I and my students were a little surprised to say the least when she said that.

"Walk with me!" she demanded gesturing me to walk out of the small classroom.

I was still waiting for her to explain herself. I took pride in my singing. I was waiting to hear the criticism she had to shower.

"How long have you been singing?".

"All my life!"

"You are such a fool!" she looked absolutely out of sorts.

"You keep saying that!". "Why exactly?"

"Well clearly you don't know you are wasting your life!"

"Excuse me?" it sounded a bit more personal this time.

"You do know that you have an incredible talent, right?" She explained after a pause.

I waited for her to say more. This could be the nicest thing I might get to hear in a while, I thought.

"It's wonderful what you are doing! There is absolutely no doubt about that. You are so young yet you are dedicating your life to all this!"

A bit of twist of fate, I chuckled. Nevertheless, I listened to her; I was interested to know what insights she had to offer.

"But we live in a selfish world Bittu! And to make life of others better first, you need to make yours better first!". I had never seen her serious anytime till today.

"What do you mean?"

"Are you saying you want to spend your entire life here teaching these kids? That's all you want to do about your talent!" She was starting to touch a cord there.

"I don't have everything figured out yet!" I said honestly.

"Have you never tried to do anything, something about it?" she asked as we walked towards the chai tapri, outside the premises of Asha.

I almost smiled at that. *I slept with a pimp of a man,* I thought!

I shook my head.

"I am going to say something and you are going to pay attention!" She demanded.

I nodded.

"I'm, correction, we are going to do something about it! I will try and make sure you get a platform better than this! I mean you can make a career out of this!"

Had this come from a man, I would have kicked him in the balls. This was different. I would have even found it difficult to digest had it come from Mallika or Arjun. But there was something honest about her.

She didn't ever feel the need to lie. That stemmed from the fact that she was very confident about herself, her place in the world, her place in other's life, she didn't feel the need to impress anyone. Hence, there was always honesty shining through her personality. All her conversations with me used to inevitably end with "we are good friends". I never paid too much attention to it. Friendship didn't mean much to me, maybe because I never had a close friend. But today she was not only promising to be one but promising to prove it to me.

She must have noticed a smile on my face.

"Trust me; you should be proud of what you are doing. But life is not all about sacrifice. It's about going after what you want, sometimes snatching it!"

Tell me about it, I thought.

That night as I lay on the bed, I couldn't get my mind off what Mugdha said that afternoon. The last few months were a slow and a gradual progress in life. I came to Mumbai with a dream but somehow the satisfaction of being able to break the shackles of my dingy house in Kanpur and doing something on my own in a new city gave me a sense of independence. I didn't fret me too much that I wasn't exactly chasing after what I had come here for! Maybe because I was a little careful after being cheated by Harry and this time wanted to make sure I give myself a bit of time.

Mugdha's word threw me right back in the middle of the web of dreams that I had spun and trapped myself in. She had a sense of purpose in her voice and I wanted to find out what was there in store for me. I didn't know yet if I believed in destiny but I was sure that she was right! I liked what I did at Asha but that was not the life I aimed for! I was building my life around a lie and if it had to be that way then might as well make sure I make it big! Or fail trying!

* * *

"You have come up with a new scheme I see!", said Arjun as we were returning home from Asha one evening. He was there for some administrative work and offered me to drop home.

I knew what he was referring to. I chose to ignore him. I saw from the corner of my eyes that he was looking at me, trying to read my face.

"You really are a bitch!" he said between his teeth. Somehow it didn't surprise me. He was always clear about his dislike for me, not vocal though.

"I told you to stay away from her, but you can't, can you?". He clearly cared about Mugdha more than anyone else in the world.

"At least I am not banging someone on the pretext of a friendship, you fucking coward!" I didn't intend to add the *you fucking coward* however, I ended up speaking my mind. He put one hand on the steering, one hand on his lips and stared back at me. There was something very intense about his looks. He spoke mostly through his eyes than mouth.

"That's all you can do, isn't it? Just stare blankly like a moron! Because you never have the right words?"

"Who I sleep with is none of your concern! But who you hurt is! Consider this a warning!"

To be honest I was afraid of him, I was always afraid of him. But somehow off late I had started answering back to him. Perhaps he was right! I had started believing Pratap Singh Bhavan to be my house.

"What is *your* story after all?" I asked.

He didn't reply.

"You got someone pregnant and didn't marry her, did you?" I teased him. He didn't respond.

I noticed he was starting to drive faster.

"Why are we taking the Expressway!" we had taken a completely different route towards the Mumbai-Pune expressway. Though I was not nervous, I didn't know where we were going. Despite all his rudeness, Arjun was not the man to misbehave with a woman. I just knew. A woman instinct! I kept quiet. I let him be.

It had started drizzling, the roads were wet and the little meter behind the steering wheel read 120. I was going a little white in the face. But I didn't dare say anything. The last thing I wanted was to distract his attention. He looked angry, lost in something. I looked at the watch; it was around eleven in the night. I looked at his cell phone kept on the dashboard. No one had called yet. But no one knew I was returning with him. I was getting a little worried.

The expressway can be quite tricky to drive on in the night, especially when it's raining. Being the connecting road between the two cities, there is always a rush of heavy vehicles at certain lengths of it, followed by long stretches of empty roads and the occasional speeding cars. But its never totally empty. It takes a winding route up and down the ghats punctuated by few long tunnels. It was getting chilly. I rolled up the window of the SUV. Finally, he slowed down, got off the road and stopped the car. I looked around. There was absolutely nothing there. It was a part of the highway which had a steep ghat on one side and huge blocks of mountains on one side. I looked around to see what the neon board above the car was! It read "DON'T STOP ON THE HIGHWAY". I was starting to freak out.

"What is it?" I asked.

"She died here!"

I was going to ask who but I stopped short. I realized who he was talking about.

Suddenly I was conscious and embarrassed about what I had said a few minutes back. I felt small, like a tiny speck of dirt in the gigantic cosmic universe. I felt like that irritating fly over the food.

"How?" I asked.

"It was night like this almost three years back in May 2002. The expressway had just been opened about a month back. She loved to drive." He paused.

I waited for him to continue.

"It was stormy. We had a fight even stormier than the night! We were arguing over something trivial. Don't even remember what it was about! I called her several times. At first she didn't answer. Then after an hour, I couldn't get through her number at all. I went to all the places in Mumbai where she used to go when she was angry. I called her friends, she had few. None seemed to know where she was. I searched for all her all night. Mallika kept on telling me to wait at the house; probably she needed some time away from me. Once she calms down, she will come back in the morning. But I was getting a strong intuition something was wrong. She was not the kind of person who would shy away from a situation. She would rather confront and sort things out. At around 6 in the morning when we didn't have any news of her, I lodged a missing report with the police."

He was talking in a low voice. He was reliving every moment. I already knew the end of the story but let him to finish.

He kept quiet for a minute. I kept on checking the road through the rear view mirror. The vision was foggy. If something would hit us from behind, we were certain to fall over the barrier into the abyss of the ghats below. I didn't want to rush him though.

"After searching for close to two days finally the police said they had found an area on the expressway which seemed to have been broken, a car seemed to have crashed into it. They were not sure but didn't rule out the possibility. We alerted the local hospitals. But nothing found! The search party tracked down the car in the valley below! It was a red Skoda." He paused.

"My red Skoda!" he continued.

His face had gone motionless. I didn't have the slightest idea why he was making himself going through the entire episode, that too for me. But my heart sank! I had tears swelling up in my eyes. He was a man of few words. I could understand what it must have been for him, not to be able to show his emotions on the face of the biggest loss of his life.

"We never found her body!" I looked at the valley beneath. It would have been impossible for anything to remain after falling from that height.

"What was her name?" I asked.

"Maaya!" That was the last word he said as we drove away from there. He had shut himself down again! I saw his cell phone ringing. It was Mugdha. He explained I was with him, caught in the traffic due to the rains.

I looked at him, he lied to her. Probably he didn't want to let her know that he was where he was. I realized that this was a place he came often. Indeed, Pratap Singh Bhavan held more secrets than I could fathom. I somehow felt there was a missing link.

*   *   *

CHAPTER 19

It would be fair to say that over time me and Mugdha had become really good friends. She was the closest I had ever been to. She was the only friend I ever had. I used to often remember my days in Ranipur Society when my so-called friends wouldn't let one opportunity slip to point out how ugly I was or how poor I was.

Mugdha on the other hand was different. She was by far the prettiest woman I had seen in my life. But she wasn't beautiful because the way she looked, she was beautiful because of the woman she was. Confident and vulnerable, brave and sensitive, loving and with conviction, rich but grounded. Every time we would go out to catch a movie or to grab a bite, she would insist I pay my own share. Her logic was that I was earning and these were ways to relish being independent. A far cry from the girls I knew at Ranipur Society who would insist on paying for me which I hated the most, pity money I thought.

She never passed a single comment on the way I dressed or looked! Not even a casual one. It hardly mattered to her. She wouldn't mind going to the mall in a pair of slippers with her hair not even tied. Such was her easy going nature. I admired that. She loved herself for she was. She loved people for who they were and not for the potential they had.

I often asked what she did for a living. She laughed at the prospect. She said her father had earned enough for her to not use the term "earn a living". It would be an insult. But she was a painter. Although I had never seen any of her work, she was particularly possessive and secretive about it. But she explained one of her main purposes to come to India was to organize an exhibition for her work, which one of her friends was helping her with.

"I have spoken to someone regarding an opportunity for you!" she mentioned in a matter of fact tone as we went out to take a walk on the Marine Drive one evening. It was raining but only just about.

"With whom?" I inquired.

"That's not important. What's important is that there is an audition for a talent show hunting for singers. It's a big opportunity as this is going to be a country wide competition. Everything is going to be aired on TV. But there is a catch!"

She paused.

"That it's just an audition and that I will have as much chance as any others?" I was sure this was the case.

"You are smarter than you let yourself believe!" she smiled.

"When is it?"

"Auditions start day after!" she explained.

She hesitated for a while and then she spoke.

"Have you ever auditioned before this?". I let out a huge laugh. She got her answer.

"You have to be prepared to face a lot of things, these things are not easy. For someone like you, its even harder, no offence!"

"By someone like me, you mean small town girl?"

"Not exactly", she was red in her face. "But yes!"

I was not offended as she was not trying to look down upon my past. Her concern stemmed from having seen the world more than me.

"I will manage! I have to give it a try!" I smiled.

We headed off for some shopping towards Colaba Causeway. Now if you are staying in Mumbai, then you have to be abreast with some of these markets. No matter how glitzy the city might look to the outsider, once you spend time here, sooner than later you will come to realize that Mumbai is a living paradox, its contradiction lives with it and breathes with it. The glamour of the money and the struggle of the common man walk hand in hand.

Colaba Causeway is an open market in Colaba that caters to everything you need. From clothes to books, jewelry to handicrafts! More importantly it's cheaper. Pratap Singh Bhavan was in Bandra, which was close to the evergreen Linking Road but we decided to walk into the narrow lanes of the Colaba Causeway. With the camera in her hand, Mugdha enjoyed capturing the colours of places like these. The concept of bargaining never failed to fascinate her as she watched as a learning student when I was bargaining with one of the vendors for a piece of polka dotted shirt. We braved the drizzles and after about an hour walked out of the market with some clothes and shoes for me, Mugdha's name on rice grain and innumerable photographs on her Canon.

We took an auto rickshaw for her ride back home. It was a distance of close to 20 kms and I took this opportunity to enquire about Maaya.

"Arjun told me how Maaya died!" I said.

She looked at me surprised. She wouldn't have expected him to share his story with me.

"That's good! He is opening up then!" was all she said.

"It's really sad, isn't it? Must have been traumatic for the whole family!"

"I don't know about the whole family to be honest." She said after a pause visibly hesitant.

"Why do you say that?"

"There was a lot of resistance to the affair!"

"From Arjun's family? Why is that?"

"Well her background didn't quite please the Singhs to be honest! I mean if I had been there in their shoes I would have my reservations too. If I didn't know Arjun as well as I do, I would have been judgmental too!" she reasoned.

"Did he tell you how they met?" she asked of me.

"No!"

She looked uncomfortable now which piqued my interest even more.

"Come on, you can tell me. I will not tell him anything!"

"Well if you do, I will not say anything to you, ever!", she said in a childlike negotiation.

I nodded.

"Well as it goes, remember I told you that after we got engaged, I moved back to New York. That was almost five years back. That's when he met her by complete chance as he insists. But when i hear about the entire episode, I can't help but think that the Universe put him there that day, because it was in his destiny to meet her. It was in her destiny to meet him." She continued like a story teller.

"You must have met that pig of a man, Harry, haven't you?" she asked me. It jolted me. Every time I heard his name, my blood would start boiling. I controlled myself from abusing him.

"Yes, Mallika's husband!" I said.

"He has had this history of being lecherous. He is downright scum bag. No morals, no way of living. Every woman he sees, he wants to shack up with them!" Disgusting I thought.

"He used to frequent this dance bar; you know the typical cheap ones! He would regularly get drunk there. Most of the nights he had to be dragged back home."

"Mallika didn't know all this?" I enquired quizzically.

"She has her own story, which she never talks about. Arjun is too protective about her. It's something he has never discussed with me either. Mallika's marriage to Harry still remains a secret. I can't believe she has had two kids with him! To think of it!" She had the same doubts as I!

"So as it goes, one night he was drunk out of control. He created a huge ruckus out there. He had his eyes on Maaya for a long time. Keeping aside what she did, she was a beautiful woman once you could look beyond her professions and three layers of artificial make up!" she said sharply.

"He was thrown out. But drunks do what drunks do! He came back with his group of men and started name calling the women there, harassing them and using Pratap Singh's name. As it turns out, one of Arjun's men was there. He called him there immediately explaining things were going out of control. But between the time he called and Arjun reached, the owners of the dance bar had lost the plot. They beat the crap out of him and his men. They were almost half dead when Arjun reached there. The goons thought Arjun was alone, so they tried to get the better of him as well. In the meantime, one of the goons shot Harry in the leg. He had missed it. Had he been on target, he would have shot in the stomach. That's when things went completely out of hand. One of Arjun's men fired at the guy who shot at Harry and managed to hit his leg. They somehow got into their car and scampered out of there. It's a miracle that Arjun and his two men are still alive.

"Basically Harry owes his life to him!" I reasoned.

"Arjun refuses to look at it that way, he probably would have done the same for anyone else but if you ask me, yes. He did save that son of a bitch."

"If he got out of there, how did he meet Maaya?" I couldn't see the link.

My mind was still screaming, *Maaya was a bar dancer? Arjun Pratap Singh's lover a bar dancer!*

"Once they reached home, Arjun opened the boot of his car to find that a woman was hiding there."

"Let me guess. That was Maaya" my mouth was open. This was straight out of a movie plot.

"Yes. Amidst all the nonsense, she had managed to get out of there and hide in the car!"

"Why would she do that?" I asked naively.

"Come on, don't be so stupid! If she didn't escape that day, she would have never been able to. She was waiting for her opportunity and she saw one. She grabbed it!"

"What happened next?"

"Of course Arjun couldn't put her up in Pratap Singh Bhavan. So he helped her lay low for a while. He had an apartment in Washi. He let her stay there for a while. The bar she worked at was closed the following day due to police raids. That meant she was out of work."

"Let me guess, Arjun like a Good Samaritan helped her on her feet"

"Well to an extent. He let her stay there but Maaya didn't want any free lunches. Whatever she did, she was independent and that's why didn't want his money, that's what Arjun insists. Arjun pulled a few strings here and there and she got a job as an assistant in a local factory."

"Interesting!"

"But as luck would have it, from the casual concern, things took a serious turn as they started seeing each other more often. Within a matter of a year, they were madly in love with each other. Arjun was convinced I was not the one for him" she smiled. I could sense that it still hurt her despite her valiant attempts at trying to be okay about it.

"He was honest with me. He told me everything! After our engagement was called off, a few months later he introduced her to his family. Pratap Singh flipped out, Mallika was furious and Harry's mis-doing was again forgotten in the eye of this storm!"

"What happened then?"

"Pratap Singh Bhavan is a mysterious place. Stories get lost here. My conversations with Arjun were limited to phone calls. One day he tells me his family is not accepting her, the next time he calls me, she was staying there. The story in between is a blur to me. But my best guess is they came around. Arjun is the only son so that helps maybe. Plus she was a good woman, a bit self-destructive but nevertheless all in all a good woman!"

"Did you ever meet her?"

"No! But she didn't get along well with Mallika. From what I know even after she agreed to her moving in, they used to have frequent fights on how she was spending Arjun's money and all. After the first few days, Maaya had started talking back too. Things were quiet ugly to be honest. But then somehow they all found a middle ground."

"What middle ground?"

"I have no idea!"

Something about the story did not add up. Maaya's accident, her affair with Arjun, her equation with the family members! It was not news to me that this family was crazy on the inside. But each day I was getting privy to the intricate details of this family.

That night as I lay on my bed, staring outside the window, my mind had wandered off to the scene where Maaya died. To the story of how Arjun met Maaya. Suddenly I was thinking of how it was to be loved by Arjun, a man of few words and even fewer emotions. I couldn't fathom how he fell in love with a bar dancer. I wondered how it felt to be in love. To love another person so completely so to forget your own identity! I was thinking about Mugdha, of her innocence, of her pretty face, of her strong will, of her big heart. I had no doubt now that she was in love with Arjun but she chose to be casual about it for his sake. Maybe he was still hurting from Maaya's loss and didn't want to be close to anyone else. Maybe he was lonely and that's why he was sleeping with Mugdha. I shuddered when my mind focused on Harry. I wondered how many lives he was to ruin. The nagging feeling of knowing there was a secret behind Mallika's marriage to him.

But come day after, I had a new challenge in life to look forward to. The audition to the talent show! I got up from my bed, opened my cup board and took out my little box of dreams, the jewelry box. I stood in front of the mirror. I had to figure out what was I going to sing. I panicked.

I decided to get to sleep. I would think about it the next day.

CHAPTER 20

It must have been eight when I woke up the next morning, the hall echoing with the aarti. But it was quite dark. I opened the window to peep outside and it was still raining. Not a whole lot but the continued drizzle!

I decided to take a day off from Asha. I wanted to prepare for the audition. I spent the entire morning choosing a song and then finally decide on a personal favourite of mine, a song called *Abhi na jao chodkar by Asha Bhosale from the hit movies of the sixties—Hum Dono.* I had sung it a few times on stage back in Kanpur and I was comfortable with it. But I was jittery. I had been preparing for this day for all my life and yet I was conscious I would make mistakes, like forgetting the lyrics, not being able to catch the tune or the beat. I didn't know who would be on the panel of judges. I didn't know how many people were coming for the audition.

I looked up the newspaper that morning and there was an advertisement announcing the details of the audition the next day. That meant a sea of people was going to the audition. Ten singers from across the country would be shortlisted for the final rounds. That meant that there was no guarantee that each center someone had to be selected. The audition was to start at 10 in the morning. The venue was listed in the newspaper. I called up the number to confirm the place. I got through after four hours. When I confirmed the time, all she said was "Be here today if you can!" I didn't really understand what she meant by that. I had never been to any auditions before and this was long before reality shows on tv became popular. So I was a little at sea to understand what to expect.

"What time do you think I should be there?" I asked Mugdha over tea that evening.

"If they say 10, be there by at least 6 or 7." My eyes popped.

"Why?"

"It's Mumbai dear! There will be more people than there are in some countries in the world. Make sure you carry something to eat, some water and an umbrella or raincoat. It's been raining for the last 2 days now".

No matter what she said or could have said, could prepare me mentally to understand what I should have been expecting. To be fair, I am certain that even she would have been surprised at what I witnessed the next morning.

*   *   *

Pouring rain, sticky mud, dirty muck, and chain of the human race as far as the eyes could see. The chaos, the cacophony, the pollution, the stench! The beads of sweat rolling down the forehead, the rain drops drenching the body! It was a sight of a lifetime! It was a chance of a lifetime! I was queued up behind at least eight hundred people waiting to get our tokens to enter inside the building where the auditions were taking place. I was waiting to enter hell and I was awaiting my turn! As I stood in that serpentine queue, someone told us that once the gates open, people would start running and there is another queue after that. This was his third attempts at audition and he said with a look of fear that he couldn't make it past the gate the last two times. My heart sank! There I stood, drenched and muddy, my legs hurting, my body tired and apparently I now needed to run a hundred meter sprint with a thousand people to get my token. That there was the realization that fair chance is only a concept. You have to fight to earn your chance as well. It's not served on a platter. My mind was wavering off to a completely different direction. It was not just about entering the building and singing at the audition anymore. It was about survival of the fittest. As much as it was about your vocal chords, it was also as much for your muscle strength. I looked ahead and I looked behind. I could see people of all kinds, shapes and figures. I started deducting who I could take on, if push came to shove! There was the thin girl ahead of me, around 10 ahead of me in the queue. She was wearing a red top and blue jeans. She looked pretty and docile. Someone I could pin down if it came to that! Then there was the young teenager, be-spectacled guy, the guy with the toothy grin, headphone plugged in his ears. I could definitely out run him. My eyes also ran on the more stylish, confident women and cocky men, whose very stance seemed to dismiss everyone else from there. It was as if no one existed around them, no one stood a chance around them. I had seen these kinds before, I had known these kinds and this was the lot I was least bothered about. I could take them any day!

I was more or less confident I could take them on! And then the gates opened, I was caught napping! All of a sudden I could hear the chaos, the splashing of muds, and the clicking of heels, the hurling of abuses, and the jostling of elbows! It was a near stampede! I couldn't fathom what was going on! Luckily I was wearing a rain coat; it saved my dress underneath from being splashed and soaked with the brown yuck mud of the ground! I turned around to see a lot of people had given up; they just stood their grounds, over powered. I couldn't figure out which crowd I belonged to, the one that was fighting each other to enter hell or the one that stood behind, outside the gates, having surrendered their chances! It was a choice I had to make and I had to make it quick.

I stood there in the middle of the near stampede, amazed at the passion of the crowd, numbed by the hysteretic scenes, feeling betrayed by the strength of my own muscles. And then I felt a powerful kick on the back of the knee and as my legs folded, I felt an elbow digging into my right shoulder. I fell down on the ground. It was as if a vicious attack was unleashed on me and I couldn't hold on my own anymore. Before I knew it, I was face down on the ground. In the middle of the ground! Flat on my belly in the pouring rain, body covered in mud trampled by thousands of feet. I felt disgusted; I could almost feel the taste of the earth on my tongue. I felt defeated. I felt cheated. I was there for a singing audition and I was put down to ground like that thin wrestler who had challenged the champion sumo. My body was beaten but my heart sank even further. My mind raced back to everything I had done to get a chance to be here, my spirit shuddered as Harry's face appeared in front of my eyes for a brief moment.

"Bittu! Bittu!" I heard someone calling my name. The voice was strangely familiar. I thought I was dying for who could know my name in this herd of animals.

The hand attached to the voice was now tapping me on the shoulder. I looked up. Now I was convinced my life was flashing in front of my eyes.

"Harry?" I asked meekly.

"Are you okay?"

"Am I dead?" I asked, his pan-stained lips close to my face. I could see his bright yellow shirt in the heavy downpour. I wondered if his shirt would turn green if it got enough sunlight and water, like the leaves. I must have been feeling lucid.

"No but pretend you are!" he whispered. *What?* I waited for him to explain.

"Don't move from here; be like this for a couple of minutes. I will get you inside!" I must have been dreaming. And then I could hear his footsteps splashing the mud, walking towards the gate, little droplets on my face, couldn't figure out if it was the rain or the mud-splash.

I had been in Mumbai for a year now and I had not spoken to Harry a single time. Not even the customary hi, not even the one—off nod of head. I treated him the way the others treated him in the house, invisible. It helped that he was not around most of the times. Now, here we were, again, of everyone out there in the world, Harry was standing in front of me. I waited to see what he had up his sleeve now. I could wait for a couple of minutes I thought.

Around exactly two minutes later, I could hear the footsteps again, splashing the mud again! Judging by the sound, I could figure there were more than two people. And then they stopped around me.

"She looks unconscious!" I heard Harry say.

"Must have fallen down when the gates opened" another voice said.

"Call Patil, ask him to get to open the medical room. Let's pick her up and take her inside!"

"Yes, fast!" urged Harry.

"The media is going to be over us like a rash if they come to know about this!" said the stranger.

I played along. I feigned I was unconscious now. I felt two hands picking me up from the ground, one hand supporting my head; a man must have been holding my legs and another one my hands. I could feel the mud subsiding on my face as I lay facing the sky now. I was hurried inside.

After incessant splashing of water on my face for 5 minutes, I decided it was time to wake up. I slowly opened my eyes to ease into the act and the scene. I saw a young boy, lanky and tall, holding a glass of water in his hand, I could see the ceiling fan above his head, wobbling and making a noise. A middle aged woman with a big *bindi* on the forehead, her spectacles on her nose, watching me with curious eyes, Harry in his bright yellow shirt, it had not turned green (*what the hell was he doing there anyway?* A subconscious thought). A couple of men, who looked like spot boys or helpers, guarded the door.

"Should we call the doctor, Madam?" asked the young lanky boy.

"Are you blind, she is bleeding, of course you need to!" said the woman in a stern voice.

The boy was almost out of the room when the woman said in an afterthought "Make sure you dodge those cameramen outside, don't want this to leak out now! We will be in trouble!"

"And that is exactly why you should think about how to make sure this doesn't get out", said Harry.

The woman looked at him curiously. She looked at me with searching looks and then glanced at him. She seemed to be doing the math in her mind.

"Let's talk outside!" she waived at him.

I saw them leaving the room. I found myself again at the mercy of Harry's hands.

*   *   *

CHAPTER 21

"Name?", asked the man sitting across the small table. I saw all the laminated plastic-number badges kept on the table. There was a microphone, a loop of wires, a register, and a laptop.

He was not looking at me. He looked to be in his mid-thirties, his receding hairline making him look a lot older than he was. He was wearing a white T-Shirt that read: "Raga—India's biggest talent hunt". My eyes lit up!

"I don't have all day" said the man. I must have been standing there quietly for more than a minute.

"I am sorry, it is Bittu!"

And there it was again! The expression of utter disbelief that followed my name! There he was, a man who must have registered hundreds of names that day and yet it did not fail to surprise him.

"You sure?" he said curiously.

I smiled at him. "I know my name!"

"I am sure you do but once I write that name here, that's the name you are going to be known by!"

"So?" I wanted to know what was it that he was suggesting! His tone was not condescending; it had the feel of advice against the pitfall that my name carried.

"You are going to be on TV baby! Even the auditions will be aired!"

At that moment, I probably didn't detest anything more than my name. Not even my father!

Then out of the moist and damp air that filled that room, appeared the name."

"Maaya!"

"Maaya it is then!" he winked as he wrote the name on one of the numbered badges—810.

"Two rooms to the right, wait your turn! All the best!" he said in one breath! I figured I was the 810th person he must have said that.

It was already late afternoon as I sat there in the waiting area outside the audition hall. There were a few others waiting there as well. All tired and their energies almost sucked out of them. The white and grey thins streams of evening sunlight was jostling through many clouds to brighten the big brown wooden window pane from across the bench I sat. I felt my buttocks twitch. I must have pulled a muscle. I should have been worried about the audition now but I was not. I looked around to see the faces of the few boys and girls to read their body language, to feel their nervousness but nothing! It had become an ordeal for most. The long queues in the rain, the arm wrestling, the chaos had sapped all of them. It looked as if most of them were wishing it to be over soon.

The strange turn of events did surprise me. I never believed much in God, to be honest, I never thought about it too much. But was there anyone up there as they say or was it my destiny that the person whom I hated the most turned up for my rescue. Harry was one of the event managers for the auditions. One of his friends had landed him up the assignment. For once, he used his pea-sized brain for my good. He made that woman, who I later came to know was one of the producers of the show, realize that this could actually boost the viewership or land the show in trouble before it was aired. He suggested they later release the tape once the show was on air to connect to the crowds, the typical videos that you see where the show subtly claims to have made the lives of so many people, of how young hearts filled with dreams and passion overcome every obstacle on their way. I didn't mind it as long as I was getting my chance. A few hours ago, I tasted the imprint of feet on cold and wet mud. A few hours later I was waiting to audition for the biggest opportunity of my life. Somewhere in my heart I knew Harry had done something he had no reason to do. I wanted to say thanks just for the opportunity if not anything else but I decided against it. I decided he was trying to clear his conscience at my expense but it was worth nothing.

A minute later the big wooden door cracked open, I could hear a voice announcing, "Maaya, please come inside!"

I had witnessed the other two aspirants who went in before me getting nervous and jittery when their names were called out. I expected the same to happen with me. But there I was, no nervous trembling of hands, no beads of sweat dropping by my forehead. Heart beat as normal as ever. May be I was over confident. Maybe because I didn't have anything to lose!

I opened the door slowly by the round metal knob and the sharp rays of the huge spotlights in the audition room scurried their way through the tiny crack of the door and the wall. I stepped inside, the huge ceilings, the musical instruments, the lights, the wires, I was enamored. I walked over to the front of the dais and faced the three judges. It felt like a dream. I had known them all my life, from the credits on the back of cassettes, records and CDs, from the interviews in their newspaper, from their appearances on tv on talk shows and award ceremonies. Only a bit different this time!

And then the legend with the curly hair waved at me to impress them in the next two minutes.

* * *

"I heard you did quite well!" said Harry as I was walking out of the building. It was still drizzling and I was struggling to open my umbrella.

I gave him a nod. I was not sure how to interact with him.

"I am going home, if you want you can come with me!" he offered. There was a definite hint of reluctance in his voice which for some strange reason I found reassuring. It was already a bit late in the night and I thought about my other options. Choose between waiting for a bus and getting a local. Neither seemed too appealing. He did help me to get an audition but I was still doing the calculation what was his interest behind it. I was very close to infer that he was pimping me out. But I refrained from letting my thoughts sway too much in that direction. I hopped on to the car.

"You shouldn't have done it!" he said all of a sudden breaking the silence after a while.

I stared back at him. I didn't care what he was opinionating about but he was the last person I would have wanted to hear any advice.

"Well, don't be surprised when Arjun flips out on finding out!" I understood what he was talking about.

"Big talks for a person who got drunk and abused her!"

He was about to say something but stopped, probably because of the lack of the right words.

"You need to be careful around here." He said finally.

"What do you mean?"

"This is a powerful family, I am sure you know that by now! And families like this take pride in their legacies, their heritage, and their so called status and go a long way to ensure that image is maintained." He spoke mincing the words.

I listened intently now. Was he hinting at something?

"Don't beat around the bush; tell me what is it that you are saying!"

"Let's put it this way" he said after a pause. "Don't make the mistake of getting too close to anyone in this family. You will hurt yourself in ways you can't imagine!'

There was no doubt left now he was warning me about something. Maybe I had gone too far in using Maaya's name. I leaned back in my seat. We didn't speak for the rest of the drive. He stopped the car around the corner of the street where Pratap Singh Bhavan stood.

"I think you should walk from here!" he suggested. He was right. The last thing I wanted was to see Mallika standing at the door and seeing us driving home together, which infact she had already seen once, in a very different way.

I was expecting someone to be waiting for me when I reached home, at least Mugdha but even she was not there. I was a bit disappointed to say the least. The last few months we had become close friends and I was itching to tell her how the day went. But she was not there. I went inside my room, a bit hungry, very tired and a whole lot more anxious. It was hard to tell at that moment what was making me more anxious. I was told at the end of the audition if I was selected, I would get a call in the next two days. Or was it Harry's not so subtle warning about the family.

I lay on my bed, trying to uncomplicated the knots. There was Asha Rani's story which was technically locked behind a door, there was the unfathomable alliance between Mallika and Harry, Pratap Singh's ebullient nature despite his wife being so sick apparently, there was the death of a bar dancer who almost married the only son of the family. To top it all there was this girl who he was engaged to, didn't marry and now was sleeping with!

I was sure I was going to complicate things a little bit more, Maaya had re-emerged and it was going to cause a flutter.

I closed my eyes to sleep and I heard a knock on the door.

"Bittu! Are you asleep?" I recognized it to be Mugdha's voice. How could I think she wouldn't turn up.

*   *   *

CHAPTER 22

"I am going to miss you!" she said with a dry smile. It was still raining the next morning. We were sitting with our cups of teas in the sheltered area of the terrace. The little droplets of rain ricocheted off the marbled floor of the terrace on to our legs as we sat on the swing.

"Miss me?" i thought she was going to talk me about being selected and going away to stay in the in-house of the production for a couple of months.

"Yes, Arjun is going to empty that double-barrel hanging in his room into you!" she said with a straight face. Turns out she was not talking about what I thought.

I knew the context was me using Maaya's name. We spoke all through the previous night. She wanted me to tell her every excruciating detail. She was all excited until I told her how I dropped the name Bittu and registered as Maaya instead. Her excitement waned then and there. She probably knew Arjun better than anybody else and she was convinced that this was going to be the beginning of a new episode of bitterness between me and Arjun.

"Why on earth couldn't you use any other name?" she asked flaying her arms after a while.

"I don't know! I was sitting there, my mind completely blank and somehow that was the only name that popped in my head!"

"And my name didn't?"

I looked at her. She had a point.

"It didn't!" I was so stupid. She started giggling. Again!

"Arjun doesn't need to necessarily know!"

"How is that going to work out exactly?" she asked curiously.

"He will only find out if I'm selected! What are the chances I might? They probably just took my audition because Harry twisted their arm and they didn't want a scene! That doesn't guarantee my

176

selection!" I reasoned. To her and myself! I must have been praying somewhere that I don't get selected. That way i would never be on TV and Arjun would never find out.

"You may be right but if you do get to be on TV, please be prepared with a reason that will be convincing enough for him to not kill you!" she said with a smile.

"I wonder though what ignited the spark of humanity in Harry out of a blue!"

"You live with a dog long enough; you will chase the stray dogs away from attacking it!" I said instantly.

It must have surprised her but as always you never knew with her! She paused for a second.

"Well, whatever it is, as long as I have known him, this is the first time I have heard about a goodwill gesture from him, so to speak!"

I was feeling inclined to tell her everything. But I held back. Not because I didn't trust her. I was afraid she would judge me. All of a sudden it mattered what she thought about me. She was the closest I had ever been to anyone. I was sure she would hate me if I told her the story about how I landed in Mumbai.

A couple of days later I got the call from the production house asking me to drop by their office.

I was excited. I was nervous. I didn't want to expect anything. But I couldn't stop reasoning with myself that if I hadn't been selected, they had no reason to call me to their office.

I didn't tell Mugdha about this. I quietly went to their office the next day.

After about waiting for half an hour the receptionist a woman came out of the office with a letter in her hand. It was the same woman who Harry was reasoning with the on the day of my audition. She had a pleasant smile unlike the other day.

She handed me over an envelope. I stood up from the sofa. I couldn't bring myself to reach out to take the letter from her hand. She sensed my anxiety.

"Don't worry, there is good news there!"

And that's how people spoil your moment. Although I was nervous and as much as I dreaded opening the letter, I wanted to find out on my own. But there she was! Grounding all my excitement!

"Read the contract, sign it and send it back by the end of this week!" By the time I looked up from the envelope in my hand, I was already facing her back.

I looked at the young receptionist who was there. She gave me a big smile.

"Your life is about to change!" she said with a big grin on her face.

I walked out of there. I had to go back to *Asha*. But I didn't. I went straight to the marine drive. I sat down on the concrete pavement, watching the dim light of the sun set behind the heavy coats of cloud. The rain had stopped but the wind had picked up. The waves of the upcoming high tide crashing against the man-made barriers, the splashes kissing my skin! I opened the envelope and held the letter in my hand, fluttering in the strong breeze. I knew the result, I should have been excited, I should have torn the envelope apart to read the letter as fast as possible but my fingers trembled.

I waited to gather my strength. There it was!

"Dear Maaya!"

My identity was disintegrating fast. Looking at the letter was looking at the mirror. Only that the reflection was not mine. It was someone else. One who bargained with middle aged married man to get out of her house. One who was using the memory of a woman who was close to a man who housed me without a reason for the last year! A not-so-pretty picture of a shallow woman, her dignity tattered, her respect muddled and her integrity amiss.

I knew I had to be ready to answer a lot of questions. My equation with the members at Pratap Singh

Bhavan could change forever. However, I had to wait and find out.

* * *

"Oh my God! You are going to be a freaking star!" said Mugdha in her usual dramatic way, exaggerating the enunciation of every word she spoke.

"Come on, that's far stretched!"

"It's not the time to be modest and humble, Bittu! Or Maaya, should I say?" she said mischievously.

I immediately turned around to see if anyone was listening. My heart skipped a beat every time she said the name out aloud. I knew it would come out of the closet eventually but I wanted to delay it as much as possible.

That night I informed the rest of the family at the dinner table that I was selected for the show. The contract required me to go and stay with the rest of the contestants in a house provided by the tv production unit sponsoring the show. There were nineteen other contestants as opposed to ten that was informed earlier. That meant the competition was going to be tougher.

The contestants were to be judged by the panel of experts however whether or not they stayed in the show depended on the number of votes they garnered each week. The entire concept of your fate being decided by the tv watchers was unnerving, especially at a time when the concept was new and was just catching the trend in the india telly circuit.

Everyone took keen interest in the concept of the show. I couldn't decipher whether it was that they genuinely took interest in what I was trying to achieve or was it that they were looking at me as a campaign booster for the next election. It was hard to tell but I didn't matter to me. Mallika particularly was keen how much of a back ground check were they going to do.

She came to talk to me after dinner was over.

"I was watching this show the other day on tv and it seems they dig up a lot of your past Bittu. You have to be careful"

I knew what she meant. My entire life was going to be built around a lie. On tiny knock and the entire castle of dreams could come crashing down like a pack of cards.

"What am I supposed to do?" I asked a bit nervous. I was confident she would come up with something. She was generally good at cooking up things.

"Well you have to play low key. You need to connect yourself with only this family. And that too when it's absolutely necessary! Cause if you stick to the version we are sticking with now, the media is going to hunt down your family in Kanpur and it's going to become a mess."

"But Mallika, they would eventually see me on tv, would they not? What if they come up here? Knowing Baba he might create a huge scene out of it?"

"The choice is simple Bittu if you think about it!" she said coldly.

"There is only version of the truth. Our version of the truth!"

There she was again! Controlling the truth about everything! I hated it. I hated her more than ever. If only I could find out what was her secret.

*   *   *

CHAPTER 23

The past always comes back to haunt us. A year ago my only concern was to get out of Kanpur. A year later I was grappling with the truth of my life. I had a choice to make. And I knew whatever choice I made now would decide how things would turn out for the rest of my life.

It was been made clear to me that if it ever came up, then the choice was simple. I had to malign my family. That I was rescued from my orthodox parents who wanted to marry me off under age. I couldn't fathom how this could turn out but I knew this was not going to augur well for them back in Kanpur. Somehow I was only worried about my brother. I knew Baba wouldn't care and mother wouldn't know what to say. And that the story will die a natural death. It could mean I would have had to sever my ties with them for the rest of my life, I life whose very foundation would be based on crucifying my parents falsely. I still felt resentment for them. It's funny how the human mind always knows to find a reason to blame something or someone to justify their own actions. The resentment I had for my parents was now based on the assumption that had they supported me, it wouldn't have come down to me being at Mallika's mercy.

On the other hand, I couldn't possibly otherwise explain how I met the Pratap Singhs and why were they sheltering me. It didn't have to reach out to the media but had Arjun and Pratap Singh found out how I landed up there, chances were me and Harry would vanish without a trace from the face of the earth. I was scared! I hated myself at that moment. I wanted to slap myself for complicating things further by registering myself as Maaya. I had no explanation for it.

It was two in the morning and I was pacing up the terrace.

"Isn't this supposed to be the night you sleep like a baby!" It was Mugdha. I could see her face in the faint light that was alit across the terrace. She had a glass of scotch in her hand, her hair resplendent in the dim glow. She was wearing a half sleeved camisole and shorts. She was leaning on the terrace railing. I couldn't help but notice her long legs, her skin smooth like butter and her perfectly shaped figure. Not too full not too skinny!

"Too nervous to sleep!' I said.

"Nervous is good, nervous tells you have something worth losing. That means you have something worth fighting for"

"Maybe!" I said. It perfectly fit the situation, what she said.

"Is it the only reason you are feeling so though?" she asked in a hesitant voice.

"Why do you ask?"

"I just get the feeling that there is more to it than you are telling me!"

I needed to talk to someone badly. At this moment Mugdha was giving me that door to open and pour my heart to her. I had no doubt that if it had to be anyone I had to share this with, it was her. She was not judgmental and all the more about me. Partly because my life was somewhat not linked to her's anyway! So it didn't matter. But it did matter to me what she thought about me. The only thing that bothered me was her proximity to Arjun. She was close to him, so close that he was like her second nature. I didn't know yet whether it was her choice to tell him everything she knew in her senses or did he hold that strong a presence in her life that he could expose her vulnerability and make her share everything with him. In any case, I was weighing my options.

"What are you saying?" I asked her instead.

"I am not saying anything! I am waiting for you tell me what's bothering you, if you want to share this with me".

I wished I had a glass of scotch in my hand too. My throats were drying up. I was going to tell her.

"You know how I came to Mumbai and why I'm staying here right?" I asked cautiously.

"Well yes, orthodox bullying parents, under age marriage and Mallika your rescue-hero, in a nutshell!" she said in a breath.

I took in a deep breath. It was time.

"Well you are right!" I paused. "Only that its load of bull shit!"

"I know!" said she sipping her scotch slowly.

I couldn't help but stare at her.

"You know?" I almost leaped out of my body.

"Well yes! I mean I don't know what's the actual story but the day Arjun told me all this, I knew you were lying. I don't believe Mallika to be a Good Samaritan and neither does Arjun. It was the part of the story that gave away." She smiled. They knew her too well.

I paused again to look for the right words. But she spoke again.

"A couple of times we have wondered though, it could be true and that Mallika was doing all this to garner some brownie points in her so called social service but then it just didn't click right. Mallika has an angle we are sure, but not sure what angle is it? I believe I will know now!" she said.

"Have you ever hated being you so much that you wished you could run away, change your name in and live in an unknown land among people who don't call you by a weird name, a guy's name and let you be?"

She was now facing me. But I looked away. It was easier that way. I didn't want to meet her eyes when I told her the truth. I grabbed the scotch from her hand.

It was almost four when I was done baring the truth about my past. I was shivering. Reliving that night with Harry! More horrified with me than with Harry! Every time I relived the night, I hated myself more, and surprisingly hated Harry a little less.

"As hard as it is to admit, anyone who might hear this might want to get Harry's head but I led him on too! Maybe I was acting stupid but I should have known!"

"Wouldn't it have been easier to just run away than to do all this?" asked Mugdha. Although she kept her voice calm her expressions were betraying her. She was definitely unsettled a bit.

"I don't know! To come from I where come from, it's a bit difficult to dream big having never set foot outside the confines our limited territories. To be honest, I was not sure about anything at that point of time. I had never been outside Kanpur, so it was all a big daze for me. The tragic twist in the tale is not me selling my innocence but thinking it would get me something in return!"

"What Harry did to you was wrong, what you did was not justifiable too, but he is a creep. He has always been a creep. Just because he helped you out the other night don't mean he is a good man. Trust me, he did that because he knows one day Arjun will find out and he will shoot him. He might kill you too but he will shoot him first!"

"He really will kill me, isn't it?" I asked meekly.

"At the moment he has no reason—but when he finds out there will be two!" This time she was not smiling.

We both knew Arjun was a sworn enemy to anyone who as much as thought about harming the family. The image of his gun tucked underneath his shirt, his fierce looks and his laconic ways scared the hell out of me.

"Do you hate me Mugdha?" I asked. I was conscious what she thought about me.

"I definitely don't hate you Bittu!" she stopped there.

"Then?"

"I don't know! It's a lot of information to process at the moment. I don't know whether to be proud of you, the way you are making your way, whether to be sympathetic towards you for being the victim, to be wary of you for being opportunistic or just be an observer in this crazy turn of things!"

"I just wish that you remain my friend!"

"As long as you are wishing, you should be praying that I don't tell Arjun any of this, isn't it?" she laughed out aloud.

"Now that you know, he might even kill you for keeping the truth away from him!" I tried to see the lighter side too.

"No he won't!" she said. She sounded surprisingly confident when she said that. She had him on the hook, I thought. Maybe he was falling for her again and she could see it.

"Your secret is safe with me dear! I won't tell him but if he asks me when he finds out the truth, I won't lie! I don't lie! Not to him, not to anyone!" she said earnestly.

I could appreciate that. She dissipated one of my biggest fears. She still wanted to be my friend and I think that day despite the big news, this was what made me happier. Mugdha was the first friend I ever had, the first person who acknowledged me as a human being, identified with my ambitions and didn't judge me by what actions I took in my past, but stuck to being my confidante.

She kissed me on my cheek and went inside. I watched her walk inside. I was suddenly jealous of Arjun.

*   *   *

CHAPTER 24

Rains in Mumbai can be very tricky as I started to find out. It was July 2005 and by each passing day in that month the downpour had been consistently heavy. It would become dark by the middle of the day, and by mid-afternoon the day began to end.

It was July 23rd, 2005. Almost two weeks after my discussion with Mugdha on the terrace. By this time whatever fears I had of losing her as a friend had subsided, or so I thought! She never broached the subject again and neither did I go near the topic. However, I did notice that she would generally avoid Mallika. Not that they were always hugging each other. But now she made it a point to show her discomfort around her. She would not sit next to her at the dining table and most of the time would get up and leave the room the moment Mallika would enter. She put on a fake smile, one that everyone knew was fake but couldn't argue against as long as she was maintaining the minimal social decorum. Goes without saying it did not slip Arjun's attention.

"What have you done now?" he demanded standing behind me in the kitchen that night after dinner.

"I don't know what are you talking about?" I ignored him.

"Of course you do! Why is Mugdha behaving so strangely?" he asked.

"How would I know? You should be asking her?"

"Don't try and act smart with me!" he demanded. I still had my back to him so tugged on my hands from behind. Almost a twist. Maybe he didn't want to hurt but it did.

"What the hell is your problem you egotistical prick!" I turned around releasing my hand off his grip. His expression didn't change. He seemed to be too angry to let that for any other.

"You don't have a problem crawling up next to her in the bed every night, but when it comes to understanding what's making her upset, you have to crawl up behind me!"

"Who I sleep with is not your concern?"

"And it isn't! Don't flatter yourself too much. But if you can do her, you sure can hell go ask her what's making her upset!" It felt as if someone else was talking in my voice. I don't know where I had found the strength from. Maybe I was getting disappointed with him. For all his macho demeanours, he still fumbled when it came to asking and answering things. He was always trying to avoid a confrontation. That irked me. What started to bother me was he was the first one to figure out the myth in my story but he never made any attempt to know what the truth was! Initially, I was under the impression he knew or was at least trying to find out what the truth was but he wasn't. He was comfortable living not knowing and I didn't have the slightest clue why it bothered me. It should have brought me relief. For someone, who was always wearing the figurative flag around the neck about protecting his family, he hardly seemed to be the one who should have been claiming it. He was always pissed at something. You could feel it. Looking at him long enough gave you the impression of an ocean that was angry but was containing within itself the huge surge of anger and resentment. Not at someone in particular but at life. Or at anything that didn't go with his flow.

"You are talking big these days, aren't you?" he spoke between his teeth after a second. He was trying to gather his composure so that he could hurt me with the most vicious verbal attacks.

"You are a leech, that's what you are. I have known too many people like you, and we have a name for them! Do you want to know what that is?" he continued. He was not going to stop today.

"We call them servants you fool! Had it not been for my sister, you would have been probably gathering dirt bags from trash cans maybe? But what do you know? You are like that ungrateful cat, you have gotten so used to living in this house, that you have made the mistake of considering yourself as one of us? Haven't you?" There was no doubt he hated me from the very corner of his heart. He believed it with his heart I was pond scum.

There was always a hint of arrogance in his voice but today it was as if he was trying to show me my place.

"Look at you all agitated as if someone has stepped on your tail?" I deliberately wanted to piss him off now. I knew there was nothing to be won arguing with him. Instead it was time for me to make him taste my medicine.

"Seems Mugdha hasn't been letting you *inside,* huh!" I mocked him. He was red with anger. If I had not known him better, I would have thought he would hit me.

"I don't know where do you get all this arrogance from? You don't have the balls to stand up for your mother!"

Whoa! I said it and I realized I shouldn't have. That was one too far.

"What?" he was gob smacked.

There was no going back now.

"You think everyone is blind. For a year I have seen Asha Rani locked in that dungeon. She is like a walking corpse. You don't so much so as talk to her. What gives you the right to talk to me like this? Big talks about family from a man who doesn't know to appreciate where he came from"

I turned to do the dishes again. My back was now facing him. I could only hear him breathing; he kept silent for a minute. Maybe he was just trying to look for the big knife to stab me in my back.

"This is the last time you have tried talking to me about her, understood?" he said

"Trust me . . ."

"Shut the fuck up and listen to what I' m saying!" he interrupted me. His voice was a like rusted knife trying cut through something thick and strong.

"The next time I hear you talk about Asha Rani or for that matter trying to run your nose in any business of the Pratap Singh Bhavan . . ." he paused.

"The world will not know you were ever born!" he finished it. He said it with sheer conviction, the air around him was pungent with resentment.

His eyes piercing me, baring me! He was threatening me cold bloodedly and I saw the side which made people pee in their pants. I really did wish I didn't push it that far. I had taken him head on and he would now look to bury me.

He was about to leave the kitchen when he stopped and turned around. He waited for me to look at him. I saw him standing at the door, brows merged together by the creases of his forehead.

Arjun Pratap Singh never ceased to surprise me.

"She is not my mother!"

And neither did he disappoint again!

It took me a minute to process the information he had flooded me with. He had already left the kitchen before I could react. I ran after him to check if he was still around. But he had already left.

Asha Rani Singh was not Arjun Pratap Singh's mother. Asha Rani Singh was Pratap Singh's wife, Mallika's mother but she was not Arjun Pratap Singh's mother. Myriad of questions spun their web around my head in a flash of a second. Was he adopted? Was he born out of wedlock? Did Pratap Singh have an affair with someone and Arjun was the proof of that. Since the time I had been in Pratap Singh Bhavan, there was not the slightest hint that he was not of the royal blood, there was not a moment when he didn't act he didn't have their blue blood running in his veins. That made even more sense. Perhaps he was Pratap Singh's son but from Asha Rani. He made it clear she was not his mother. Where was his mother? How did a woman like Mallika love her step brother so much? Everything that I had seen and come to believe in the last few months had gone away. One little information and all my assumptions and study about the family were washed away. Did Mugdha know too?

The more I thought about it, the more I was convinced she had to know. She lied to me. Actually she didn't! As always she didn't tell anything she was not asked. Convenient! Indeed, this house held more secrets behind its towering walls than one could imagine. Each time, I was made privy to information that I shouldn't have been to! Of all the questions, one thing that should have and didn't appear in my head was, why of all the people in this whole wide world, he would choose to tell me that Asha Rani was not his mother. Was he playing me? I didn't want to but I had to find out.

*   *   *

CHAPTER 25

The incessant rains had paralysed life in the city. Pratap Singh had decided to spend time in his office in the house. His associates dropped by numbers the next day, 24th July. They stayed through breakfast, lunch, tea, dinner! The house-helps were muttering their wits out. It was a challenge to cater to so many guests at short notice, that too when it had been raining so heavily. Having to go out to buy groceries would mean having to get drenched. It didn't amuse them. Pratap Singh and Mallika always wanted the house to be spick and span. The dirt and the mud the shoes carried inside, there had to be someone on standby near the entrance to make sure it was immediately cleaned up. Circus was the word that came to my mind.

Mallika was in her room most of the day with the kids. One of the rare occasions that she spent time with her children! Harry had parked himself in the garage for most of the day, doing something or the other with the cars. Arjun was in the recreational side of the house, spent the morning in the pool with Mugdha, played snooker with his two friends and had been in that room playing cards with them most of the day. He had walked past by me a couple of times. We didn't make any eye contact. But every time we passed each other, there was this unexplainable tension between us. I had goose bumps.

Ever since the time he told me about her not being his mother, my mind was fixated on that. I was trying to observe every nuance, every interaction between the rest of the family members and Arjun. I even put Mugdha under scrutiny. But I couldn't figure anything. It was stupid of me to even think of finding any answers in there. This was a family with political roots so deep that if one had to pull it out, it would come out from the other side of independence era. Of course that meant their behavior was always polished, their words measured and they took immense effort to appear effortless.

Late that night after dinner, Mugdha came over to my room. Arjun's friends had just left. He had gone straight to bed.

"I think he had one drink too many tonight!" she said as she folded her legs and rested her head on her elbows.

"Never seem him drinking!" I commented casually. I didn't know if Arjun had mentioned anything to Mugdha about our conversation the last night.

"Doesn't drink much these days! He is allowed once in a while!" she sounded like his wife. I had no clue why they weren't married.

What Arjun had told me the day before it has started bothering me! It didn't to the bit amuse me. I had no business in their life and despite the entire rebuke that I got from him; I felt this great itch inside my head to find out what was the true story behind all this.

Mugdha had been talking about something. Her days in U.S.! It was general girl gossip and my mind had wandered off. After a while when I turned my attention towards her, she was still turning the glossy pages of a fashion magazine and talking! This time about how out of place she felt in college because apparently she was a bit clumsy!

Like anyone would believe that!

I placed my hands on her hand in an effort to make her stop talking. I had to ask her. The time had come.

"Mugdha?" I shook her hands.

She turned towards me. My face must have looked extremely serious cause she didn't say anything but looked at me curiously waiting for me to say what I had to say.

"I want to ask you something and promise me you won't lie!" that probably was not necessary. She never lied anyways.

"What is it?"

"Do you know that Asha Rani is not Arjun's mother?"

She sat up.

"How did you find out?" was all she could mumble.

"Is that important?" I asked.

"Yes it's important!" she almost shrieked out.

I was taken aback by her reaction. She obviously knew and had intended to keep it a secret.

"Well, Arjun told me last night!"

"Arjun?" she shrieked again. Utter disbelief on her face!

"Yes!" I said in a low voice. I knew I had to weigh my words now.

"We had a fight the other day and we both said each other some things.

"That is so strange!" she seemed confused. "Arjun never mentions this to anyone!"

"Well he was angry at me and wanted me to stay out of his business. Anyways he must have told you! He knows I won't mention this to anyone!" I was trying to reason.

Mugdha was looking straight at me. She was wearing an expression that was a bit hard to read. If I didn't know her well I would have thought she was angry at me.

"All these years, he has not said anything to me!" was what she said after a while.

My jaws dropped.

"What do you mean hasn't said anything to you? How do you know then?" I asked curiously.

"Promise me not to tell Arjun about this? Or anyone for that matter?" she said her voice low.

"Maaya!"

"Maaya?" I screamed out so loud that she put her hands on my mouth.

"Are you crazy?" she said between her teeth. My eyes were popping out.

"You have no clue what kind of information you have become privy to!" she said. She was looking more and more intense with each passing minute, with each word.

"I didn't become privy to anything that I wanted to! What new shit is this? He told me on his own! Will you stop freaking out and tell me what the matter is?" I said, trying hard myself not to freak out.

"When Maaya passed away, I visited Arjun, to be at his side! I had stumbled across one of her journals in his room!"

"You read it?" I asked incredulously

"What do you mean you read it? Of course I read it. It was the journal of a dead woman who died in mysterious circumstances!"

"What did it say?"

"Well she had been staying at Pratap Singh's for some time when she started writing the journal it seems! In the beginning it was all about how beautiful this house was, how glamorous the life was how amazing it was to be his fiancée. The regular being enamored stuff! She was not a keen writer, from what I could understand. She was definitely not a woman who would keep a journal!"

"Did that not strike you weird? From whatever I know about her, she didn't sound to me either as well as someone who would account her daily life just for the love of writing!

"Exactly what I thought! That meant only one thing. The first few pages were bluffs. She had picked up writing the journal because she too was becoming privy to information that someone wants to keep behind these walls!"

"When you say information you mean Arjun not being Asha Rani's son and when you say someone you mean Arjun right?" I asked.

"The first bit correct, the second I'm not sure! I have absolutely no part of me that thinks Arjun played dirty. He didn't need that! He wouldn't have let her in his house then!"

"As the journal goes on, her writing becomes more and more vague. Not just her hand writing which progressively deteriorated but the lucidity of her thought process. The journal stopped making sense to me. It was more and more puzzling. Bunch of words and not coherent sentences! It was as if she wanted to write but her mind wouldn't allow. Almost as if her mind was disintegrating!"

"Was she going mad?"

"I wouldn't go that far! She had pictures from exactly the same time. She looked absolutely fine in those. I even spoke to Arjun to find if he figured something was wrong. But nothing! Not even the maids noticed anything different."

"In one of the pages amongst multiple pages of gibberish, she mentions one coherent sentence. Arjun is a bastard! At first I thought she had a fight with him and called him names! But a few pages later for the first time she talked about it more in detail.

"Where is the diary?"

Mugdha paused for a min.

"It's still with Arjun!"

"Shit!"

"I have a copy!" she said.

"What?"

"I didn't know what to do when I found it out. I had only one day in hand and I had to read it. I couldn't dare to take the original one. Had Arjun even spilled a single word about a missing journal, I would have been inside a coffin by now! I did what I thought was smarter! I photo-copied the entire thing."

"Where is the copy?"

"It's in my room!"

"Have you lost your mind?" her's was the guest room.

"What's wrong?"

"You left that in the guest room! What if someone goes through your stuff?"

"Don't be mad at me but I think someone already tried to! I had kept the suit case on the right side of the cupboard and I found it on the left side one day!"

"Whoever it is knows about the copy then?"

"I don't think so cause I had kept it in the bag and it's locked! I always carry the keys!"

I breathed a little bit.

"Go get it the journal, let's read it!" I told her.

"What? You mean here?"

"Yes!" I looked at her; bewildered that she didn't think of it.

"Give me two minutes!" she sneaked out of the room quietly, closed the door behind her. I sat on my bed impatient. She came back after a couple of minutes. The moment she walked inside my room the lights went off.

"It's the rains! I think I heard one of the transformers go off!"

It sure had. I stumbled across the table to light a candle. Mugdha lit a cigarette.

We crouched down on the floor next to the bed. I had pulled the curtains.

"Be quite!" she said.

We had to keep our voices down. The lights going off meant it was silent like a graveyard. We were not sure if someone was listening to what we were talking about. We were whispering.

I took the copy of the journal in my hand. Mugdha had taken efforts to maintain it. It was bunch of papers stapled together in order. She had kept it covered with a plastic. As I turned over the pages, it seemed I was reading an attempt at a comic book by an eight year old kid. The writing was clear and distinct in the first pages. She had clearly started writing the journal in hindsight and not as part of a habit. There was meticulous description of the house members, of their routines. She was a keen observer. After roughly about thirty to forty pages later her writing started to deteriorate. As Mugdha said it was drastically vague and strange and a bunch of drawings across pages. I had been carefully reading it as Mugdha kept on smoking, one cigarette after other. She was on her third when I finally came across what was probably one of the most shocking parts.

"The day is dark not because it hides behind the clouds but because the shadows people cast over other's lives. So many years she has nurtured a son not her own and given him the love that a mother can give to her child. But the pain Asha must be going through to raise the child of one of my kinds. But the walls are mighty and they will hold this secret within their heart. No one will know the dirty politics this family has played. He is a good man! He doesn't have to suffer. Maybe it's for good. May be it's not! Will he get his due? Will he get his rights?"

My heart had stopped. I couldn't breathe. What did she mean child of one of my kinds?

I looked at Mugdha. She had a tear rolling down her face.

"Fucking shit!"

*　　*　　*

CHAPTER 26

My mind had started going into a tizzy. I couldn't believe what I was reading! It had to mean only one thing.

Arjun Pratap Singh was not Asha Rani's son. But I am sure his life would have been a lot easier if that was the entirety of the truth.

I looked at Mugdha.

"Arjun's mother was not like Maaya. Maaya was a bar dancer. His mother was a hooker!" she said.

"Maaya was probably just being polite when she wrote that down!"

"How do you know? Does she mention that anywhere?" I asked curiously.

"Well you know, the media takes a certain interest in these political families. There was one such guy called as Raju Kumar, a young enthusiast working for a hindi newspaper. He had been a great fan of Pratap Singh for a number of years and started writing a biography tracing his roots. Pratap Singh was fond of the man, there was no reason not to be; he always had good things to write about him. Poor bastard started running his hand too deep in the shit and couldn't come out!"

"What do you mean? Was he murdered?"

"Well he died in an *accident*!" she said air quoting accident.

"How do you know all this?"

"I have contacts! I belong to a family with network wider than this family honey!" she said in a matter of fact tone. She had no reason to lie.

"These things die down after a few days but there is always some trail. After he died I came across some of his documents in his house which linked Arjun's birth to a woman named Seema who died in the hospital during child birth. Her time of death exactly half an hour later to Arjun's time of birth. Same hospital! Same room! There was only 1 woman admitted in that room that night! It had to be her! Seema was Arjun's mother!"

"Call me crazy but the fuck where you doing at Raju's house?"

"Well I came to India after a few months of his death, after Maaya passed away. It was my first trip to India after moving to U.S. Arjun mentioned about this guy. I found something was fishy. I decided to look around a bit. My cousin is a journalist. He helped me dig up a bit."

"Does Arjun know you nosed around all this?"

"Well in the beginning he didn't know! I told him later death though. He deserved to know who all were aware about the biggest secret of his life! That's how I know without Arjun mentioning anything to me."

"What about Mallika and Pratap Singh?"

"Do you think I would have been alive till now? Arjun made it clear to me that if I wanted to live no one could know that I was aware of all this!"

"He doesn't trust them?"

"It's not a question of trust! It's a complicated thing! He doesn't know who killed Raju, he doesn't want to find out either. But I guess he suspects if he digs deep, he will find the answer he doesn't want to. They both love Arjun to death!"

"Please don't tell me Arjun is seeking love in the fact that someone was murdered to make sure he doesn't get hurt?"

"Yes!"

"That's bull shit!" I almost shouted out.

"If Raju was killed that was not because of their love for Arjun but to make sure they could bury the secret of the family. Obviously Arjun Pratap Singh didn't want anyone to know that he fathered a child from a prostitute!"

Mugdha didn't say anything. She knew I was right.

We both kept quiet for a moment.

My head buried in the pages a new theory had started weaving its web around my mind. There was no doubt left now that Maaya knew things about the family that was not pleasing someone in the family. It was the cause of discomfort maybe for one, maybe for all in the family.

"Maaya did not die in an accident, did she?" I said it aloud finally after thinking hard for a while. It made more sense when I said it aloud. I could see the twos and twos adding together right in front of my eyes.

Mugdha opened her lips to say something but then held back to find the right words.

"Who do you suspect?" was what she replied with. Clearly, the thought was on her mind too. She must have suspected it too. Else there was no reason to go through all the trouble to keep Maaya's journal, to find out about Raju and what he had dug up. I could see from her face that we both were thinking the same thing.

"I don't know yet. I mean obviously Pratap Singh seems to have the most legit motif but tell me who are you thinking about?"

"I have always worked on the deductive theory to understand this bit. I have no doubt it was someone within the family. Maaya seemed to have lost all touch with the murky people from her past. Plus her alliance with a man like Arjun meant no one would dare touch her. Even the goons from the bar who Arjun picked up an enmity against!"

"Let's not completely disregard the theory. Put a pin on it for now!" I didn't want to rule out the possibility of her ex employers being hired to do the dirty job.

"Points the gun to this family then! Who was she not close to?"

"Well she was only close to Arjun I believe!" she said.

"Make no mistake Pratap Singh and Mallika had a fondness for her too. At least that was the image that the world had!"

"What about you? What do you think?"

"I think they both hated her to the gut and even if they didn't do anything, they are happy that she is not around anymore!"

"Doesn't that mean one of them might be involved?" I asked. I was thinking hard now.

"Yes it does! But it's hard to point a finger at anyone because nothing seems to tie up them up. Maaya's phone records could not be found. The police never disclosed them. The car was damaged beyond a point they couldn't figure if there was anything wrong with the mechanics of it. So that rules out the possibility of an accident. Even it was, the question remains, did someone play dirty with the car?"

"What about the diary? You must have read it so many times, haven't you been able to link something up!"

She kept quiet for a minute. It seemed again she was looking for the right words.

The burning candle, the silence of the night and the lead to solving a death had started giving me a heady feeling. Mugdha was a woman who always had a smile on her face. Tonight I had forced her to think some things which she clearly didn't like. She obviously had tried solving this on her own but she hadn't found the answers to her questions. I just wanted to know the truth. Suddenly there was an element of mystery and tragedy around Maaya's death.

As we sat there trying to figure out the missing link, something came to my mind. That night when I had tip toed outside of Asha Rani's room. I had head Mallika talking to her in a threatening voice.

"What about Mallika? Have you considered her?"

She looked right at me. Almost as if I asked her a silly question.

"Do you not know her yet?" she asked with a bit of contempt I thought. More for Mallika than for me!

"That's why I'm asking you" I said.

"Mallika takes pride in her lineage. She has gone to great lengths to keep the legacy of this family alive. Every word she speaks, it drips in the blue blood ego pool. She is the Mafia of this family. Not Arjun! Arjun is the watch dog! But I have always felt that the leash is in her hands. She is the commander of this Singh family, discretely planning every move, making sure everyone does what she wants! All this for what? The status, the image of the family! Ask me if you will, she is the puppet master. That woman is toxic. She has politics running in her vein."

"Do you think she plotted with Pratap Singh to have Maaya removed?"

"I think she is on her own on this one" her answer was not ambiguous this time. Each passing moment, with each answer she was more and more confident that Mallika had plotted Maaya's accident!

If I was not up until now, I was scared to hell now. A sudden flashback started replaying in my head. The day she found me with Harry, the calm reaction and then making sure I vanished without a trace from Ranipur Society in the blink of an eye. It all seemed immaculately planned yet in so much little time. Getting me out of there ensured that I didn't get to make any noise about it even if I wanted to. Thus making sure the scandal didn't come out and tarnish the name of the family as Harry was linked to this family. Then portraying the story that she rescued me! Giving me a place to stay in the same house! Even if the truth came out ever, people would talk about her generosity. Winner again! If it didn't, that would be because I would be grateful enough to her for saving my life! Winner again!

It was so elaborately planned that no matter what happened the Pratap Singh Bhavan's image had no scope of being tarnished. Thereby making sure the legacy built of for years stayed alive. So was that the reason Asha Rani was locked in a room, and Maaya was sitting pretty in heavens now.

CHAPTER 27

There was something about the continuous downpour of the rain. It was not tearing down with vengeance from the heavens but in a very insistent way was carrying on its business as if it was on a mission. It was past three in the morning. The room was getting congested with the cigarette smoke, the damp smell of the lawn outside, the background score of the rain drops on the tin roof of the servant quarter across the house. Pungent was the ambience as every page of the copy of Maaya's journal seem to be unearthing some hideous faces of the Pratap Singh Bhavan.

"Do you know if Arjun ever read that journal?" I asked.

"The funny thing is he never mentioned it to me. I took it out for a few hours and placed it right where it was after I had taken the copy"

"So we don't know if there is anyone else who knows about the journal?"

"I suspect there is! I suspect it's one of the two between Mallika and Pratap Singh!" she said.

"I think its Mallika!"

"How are you so sure?" she asked.

"Do you not know her?" this was my turn to say that. She smiled.

"That woman is plotting every single moment of her life! Not only her life but other's as well!" I didn't realize then but Mugdha's judgment of Mallika a few minutes ago had a profound impact on my views on her. Not that I held her high in regards in anyways but knowing she felt the exact same way, it made it clear that Mallika's hands might have been red with Maaya's blood.

I was filled with rage and contempt. It all started making sense to me.

"Mallika might have been little when Asha Rani adopted Arjun as her son. She for that matter must have been unaware of the entire episode for the good part of her life. Until Raju showed up!"

"Until Raju showed up!" she repeated.

"Raju had started digging up the dirt on this family. It started out all good with him eulogizing Pratap Singh and making him look like a hard working hero. Soon he was into unknown territory. He had gained access to the closet where Pratap Singh hid his skeletons."

"That's when Mallika must have come to know about Pratap Singh's mistress; Arjun's mother!"

"Raju must have told Mallika about this and this must have absolutely shattered her ego!" she said.

We both kept quiet for a minute. Both trying to picture the look on Mallika's face! How her blood must have boiled when she would have come to know that the blue-blood anthem she would chirp all day long was just a scandal, that she was as ordinary as any others, that Pratap Singh was a philanderer. That Arjun despite her pride was not born of the same mother.

I had seen that look on her face. That look of utter loathing, but not a word said. The veins popping in the forehead but not a finger trembling! It's the action, not the reaction that was to be feared. She had her way. She had it with me and I was certain she had it with Raju.

"Oh my god!". Mugdha too had done the math.

"I think Mallika had Raju killed too!"

There, I said it.

I looked at the watch. It was almost four in the morning. I walked over to the window of the room. That was the best part about the room. Its huge wooden framed window; the glass impeccably clean and transparent. The rain drops slid on the glass. The view unclear! I could see that the roads were starting to get water logged. It had not stopped raining since the previous night. Looking outside the house I realized the entire area was enveloped in darkness, there was a power trip for sure.

"How are we ever going to prove all this?" I turned around and asked Mugdha.

"Whoa! Wait! What?" she was taken aback by what I said.

"We need to uncover this, don't we?" I was surprised by her reaction.

"I am not too sure yet! I mean this is a major scandal, but I really don't want to be at the receiving end of a bullet or a knife or for that matter be buried alive!"

"You can't be serious! We are smelling murders here and you are talking of doing nothing!"

"We don't have any proof yet, ok! Whatever we have arrived at, it's merely based on a few frayed loose ends and mostly assumptions!"

"Doesn't matter, some day we might just piss her off and have a good chance of being buried right here on this lawn! The dogs will come and pee on you!" I said, absolutely in dismay that she was not willing to do anything about all this.

"If you do want to nose around, then you are just making sure that does happen!" she exclaimed.

"Bittu, this is not your run of the mill average next door family. This is daily life for people like them. I have grown up with this family. I have seen them, for that matter, even my family; do things that people will find bizarre. But they do it and get away. It's not a co incidence. It is because they know how to get out. You try and harm them; they make sure your name disappears from the pages of history. They won't think twice." She looked serious.

"I know them too well Bittu! The more you try digging around, the more trouble you are calling for yourself!"

"Then why have you bothered yourself for so many years!" I asked.

"I had to know! I have been with this family for too long. But I haven't tried doing anything crazy" she said.

"You cant claim to be close to Arjun if you don't want to bring him peace!" I don't know why I said that.

She was about to say something but stopped.

"I do my bit!" she said turning her face away.

"You think it's easy going to bed with a man knowing I was never his first choice! I have chosen to look beyond that. For his sake! Why do you think I have been staying here all this while? I hate this family more than any one does, I'm here only for Arjun!"

I couldn't argue with her after that. It must have been heart breaking for her to be in love with a man who was nursing his wounds over losing his fiancé. She never showed the part of her that was hurt but it was not difficult to understand. She had known him forever. Arjun took her for granted. He was too close to the picture to be able to see that she was the one he was meant to be with! She had given up her life for him. He didn't see that, it was sad!

She lay on my bed. She was trying to tuck the pillow under her head but her huge curls kept throwing her head off. It was almost cute watching her struggle to tie them up.

"You have the most beautiful hair!" I said to her.

"I know!" she giggled.

That was the Mugdha I had become so fond of. Always happy! But as she pulled the bed sheet over her head and went to sleep, I stood there in a haze. This was not normal. I couldn't possibly sleep knowing there had been two murders that this family was involved in! Mallika's face was like a background in the maze of images. I went and lay next to Mugdha. Knowing not what my next step should be when I wake up from this sleep! I was sure of one thing though, whether or not I did anything about it was a different question, but I had to get to the bottom of all this. How close I was to solving this puzzle was not clear to me! Though I knew I was very close! My heart was speaking to me that despite the entire link that we connected there was something still missing.

As I saw her sleeping peacefully without a worry in the world despite all that we discussed made my mind pregnant with another thought! This was a nagging thought that had popped its head somewhere in my consciousness. I kept on pushing it back. I was too afraid to acknowledge it. If I did, I had to follow my intuition and I was too afraid of being right! I was afraid of losing something I didn't have yet!

I closed my eyes uncertain what the morning held for me. All of a sudden I was picturing the simple life back in Kanpur. Away from all this complications! All I wanted was to follow my dreams. This is hardly the path I wanted to take.

It was like reading a paperback novel, each page unfolding a new mystery at a pace I couldn't keep up with. I wished I had my brother with me! He would know what to do! Was I missing my family? Think I was.

* * *

CHAPTER 28

We woke up around nine. I saw Mugdha standing next to the window. She was smoking. I think that was what woke me up.

"Good morning!" I said rubbing my eyes.

"It's like the heavens are crying!" she said. I figured it must have been still raining.

I got up and went next to the window as well. The streets were water logged. There were a couple of men walking past the house carrying their belongings on their head. I noticed the water was well above their sheen. The sky was dark! It was hardly a morning. It looked like a late afternoon. The electricity was not back yet.

"I think we didn't have the aarti today!" I said. No one had woken us up.

"We should go outside. I will go to my room. Need to take a shower!" she said. She went out of the room.

I noticed she spoke as if nothing happened. She was her usual self. It was almost unusual. I couldn't imagine how she could be so calm about everything. I had definitely lost whatever peace of mind I had left in me.

I went to the hall after about half an hour and saw the entire family at the breakfast table.

"I haven't seen the water logging like this since decades!" exclaimed Pratap Singh as he munched on his toast. Arjun was sitting next to him. He was wearing a half sleeved gym shirt. I couldn't but help notice his arms. His triceps were so well defined you could count them. He quietly ate his breakfast. Mallika was trying to get her daughters to eat. Not a worry on her face! I wondered how these people could behave so normally. It was disgusting. The water melon juice on the table and I could think of Raju's and Maaya's blood. Was this what it took to be rich and famous? At the cost of morality! At the expense of someone's lives! Living in a world where nothing mattered, no one mattered.

At this point one of the servants came running inside with Harry. He looked tired and wet!

Arjun immediately got up from his chair and went to them.

"What's the matter?" he asked.

"Half of Mumbai is flooded!" Harry panted.

"I went down to the market early to get some groceries and I was stuck in my car for more than an hour! The doors were jammed so I couldn't even get out. Thankfully Kishan here was passing by, with the cycle on his head, he saw me and helped me out."

Mallika didn't even get up from her chair but the kids ran to their father.

"The entire area is flooded! We need to empty the servant's quarter. The water is rising up and before we know it, the area around the house is going to be sub merged."

That alarmed everyone.

"We would need to move everything on the first floor!" said Pratap Singh.

I didn't realise it was that bad. I ran to the terrace to see what the situation was. I grabbed an umbrella and the moment I opened the door, a fierce gush of wind almost knocked me off my stance. I went to the western side of the terrace and saw something I will probably never forget in my life. There was water as far as the eyes could see. The lower areas around the colony, towards the northern end of the road were already submerged. The slums were floating in the water. People were struggling to walk as the level of water kept on rising. I was scared to death.

The southern end of the road, there was a wave of water coming as if it was a river. Bikes stuck, cars jammed, a couple of kids were swimming to get across, a small boy had climbed up the tree nearby. I had never seen a flood in my life. I didn't want to die like this.

"Bittu!" I heard someone screaming.

It was Mallika.

I ran inside.

"Move out your stuff from the room!" she mentioned and started walking off.

"Where to?" I asked.

"In my room!" she waved.

"What?" I screamed out.

She turned around, not amused.

"Do it fast, we need to move the empty the ground floor!"

I couldn't protest that! This was probably the last day of my life, this way or that.

I ran downstairs. Arjun and Harry were moving the furniture up the stairs into the recreation room. That was the first time I had seen them together. Mugdha was nowhere to be seen. I noticed her door was still locked.

For the next half an hour every member in the house was running around. Some moving the furniture, some gathering the groceries from the kitchen, some filling up buckets of water! Clearly some of them had been in situations like this and they thought it was wise to stock up.

"I have no clue what to do with the cars!" said Harry.

That clearly was a problem. There were 5 cars and surely you couldn't move them anywhere!

"Move them to the garage, I will make a barricade with the sandbags outside the door" said Arjun.

"Make sure you move everything inside and don't lock the doors. Shut the windows" he said calmly.

It was surprising how he could keep his head in a situation like this when everyone was panicking. Harry moved the cars into the garage.

Arjun locked them down, then carried the sand bags from the storerooms and piled them up in front of the garages. Then he and Harry helped the servants empty the quarters and move them into one of the spare guest rooms on the first floor. For all their heartlessness, there was one rare moment of humanity. I was standing in the lawn with an umbrella over Arjun's head. I saw Mugdha standing at the window of her room. I couldn't clearly see her face. She had closed the curtains the next time I looked up; I thought she must have been coming down.

When I went inside after sometime, I realized she had not come out of her room. It was unlike herself. I went up to her room. I knocked before I entered.

"You don't have to knock!" she smiled as she opened the door.

I saw she had packed a small bag.

"What's that for?" I asked pointing at the bags.

"A few essentials" she said.

"I like to be prepared!" she smiled.

She was combing her hair.

"I think you should too!" she said. She was right. The problem was my stuff was in Mallika's room. Why hadn't I said no to her and moved into Mugdha's room?

"Can I stay in your room?' I asked Mugdha.

"I thought you were going to anyways, weren't you?" she looked surprised.

"Yes I was!" I went to Mallika's room to move my things again.

She was sitting on the chair. She saw me pick up a bag and head out.

"I am not that scary, am I?" she asked without looking at me.

"Excuse me?" I didn't hear her properly the first time.

"You can't spend a day with me, can you?" she asked.

Why the hell was she asking me all this? I was turning white with anger. The more I looked at her, the more she seemed like a mafia to me.

The thing about fear is you hardly feel it around someone who is kicking and screaming around. It's always the lull before an impending storm, the one that slowly creeps up, silently spreading through your lungs, choking you up, and stops you from breathing! Mallika always gave the impression of her being the silence before the storm. You could never guess what was going on in her mind. There was no impulsive actions in her life. Everything was pre meditated, planned and plotted, start to finish. From choosing her clothes, to choosing the people she wanted around her; every decision weighed against and thought about.

"I don't want to crowd you!" I could mutter somehow.

"In that case you can stay in her room. Don't have to move around your luggage. Keep it here. Come in whenever you want to!"

I didn't say anything. I couldn't figure out why she was being nice to me! Was it her play! Be nice to the victim before you push them off the edge.

I met Mugdha in the corridor. She was on her way to the kitchen.

"Going to grab a bottle of water, I'm going to be up here all day, so what the hell!" she said as she trundled down the stairs.

I went into her room. I noticed how clean and organized it was! There was not a single object that lay scattered out of its place. Everything in impeccable order! I hardly ever had been to her room.

I couldn't but help notice that her passport was out on the desk. It was silly of her to keep it there. I picked it up to put it inside the drawer. I never held a passport and out of curiosity opened it. I noticed the first page was where our details are; followed by the pages of the visa stamps. As I was flipping through the pages, knowing that even if Mugdha came in, she wouldn't mind me going through it; I came across a page that read Mumbai airport stamped 15th May 2002. I stopped on it for a second. I flipped forward. I noticed 10th Dec 2001.

Seemed odd! I tried recalling what Mugdha told me about her visits to India. I could remember her saying that when she visited Arjun after Maaya's death, it was after a lot of time, in fact her first trip since she moved from India. Five months hardly seemed too much time. Did it slip out of her mind? Of course it would have. But surely she would have remembered considering she was coming home for the first time since leaving India.

I heard her coming up the stairs. She was talking to someone on the phone. I kept the passport where it was and walked over to the other side of the room.

"It's ok dad! I'm fine. I will be there tomorrow when the rain stops!"

"Its my father!" she said after she hung up.

"He wants me to go over to his place, as if I'm going to swim across all this water!" she said sarcastically.

I was about to ask her about the trips to India which I saw on the passport but I didn't. It didn't seem like a good idea to tell her I went through her passport.

We instead decided on a game of cards.

We sat there playing cards for hours. The rain got heavier and we could see the water level rising, slowly flooding the servant quarters. It was a scary sight.

The electricity poles were floating on the water, the bus stand nearby was perilously holding on its last foot and as I saw how a car was submerged in the water, a huge branch of tree came crashing down on it. Arjun and Harry were screaming from the porch outside to check if there was someone inside the car. Thankfully no one was! The day had gotten dark, the clouds menacingly grey promising to tear open its belly and drown the mighty city. From the room nearby, we could hear the radio. This was by far the worst rain-hit crisis the city had been in decades. People were not ready and were left stranded wherever they were. Offices were shut by two in the afternoon, public vehicles were immobilized and hundreds were stuck nowhere, between their offices and home.

"I am glad we didn't go out today!" I said. "It would have been fun!" she replied.

"Fun? Yes, swimming across in puddled water is not my idea of fun!" I said

"I'm hungry, let's go check what's to eat!" she walked out of the room.

I went to Mallika's room. I don't know why!

CHAPTER 29

There was hardly ever a time when Mallika was not occupied. She would always be in a hurry so it felt unknown when I entered her room that day and found her resting. Even on that gloomy morning when life had come to a halt she looked impeccable, hair tidily held back, wearing a black shirt and tracks with her head resting on the easy-chair!

I cleared my throat so that she knew I was in the room. She opened her eyes, saw me and closed it again.

I stood there for a minute not knowing what to do.

"Sit here!" she gestured on the chair next to hers. The room was poorly lit, only by the small window across the room allowed the dim light of the day to penetrate.

I sat down, a bit reluctant, so many things on my head. Angry and scared at the same time! I prayed I didn't say anything that shouldn't.

"Don't worry, everything is under control!" she said calmly. She was talking about the rain and the water logging. She could have been talking about anything else as well.

"Have we checked with anyone how things at Asha are?" I asked not knowing where to start.

"Yes Aaji had made arrangements; most of them have been moved to the trust's building on the third floor. It's all fine!" I was glad to hear that.

"Times like this you realise how insignificant we are, isn't it?" she said staring at the ceiling.

I nodded.

"Insignificant and alone!" she lingered on the word alone.

"Alone? You are surrounded by friends, family, people who worship you and people who are scared of you!" I said.

She looked at me.

"You are one of those who are scared of me, aren't you?" she said with a wicked smile.

"No I'm not!" I said sternly. I was looking at my feet when I said that. Didn't make a good impact I suppose for she burst out laughing.

"You are! You are!" she repeated as she was laughed hard.

"I would want to know why though?" she asked with earnestness.

I paused for a moment. There was no pretending with this woman.

"After all I have done for you, you don't even look me in the eye and talk" I would have sworn there was a hint of rue in her voice.

"You have always made it clear that I don't belong here!" I said.

"You have been here over a year now!" She had a point.

I couldn't argue that.

"I suppose you and Mugdha are good friends!" she said.

"I think so!"

"That's good! We all need friends!" she said.

"Can I ask you something?" she asked.

"If you become successful, what would you be most thankful for?"

That was a tough question. I had never thought of it. Guess somewhere I would have had to be thankful to her for pulling me out of Kanpur, no matter how twisted her interests were.

"I suppose for the opportunity that I got!" I said.

She smiled. I was sure she got her answer.

The tea pot was set on the table. I went over to pour her and me some. I could hear Mugdha laughing downstairs. That meant I still had some time to talk to Mallika.

"I know about Arjun!" I said without a preamble. It didn't startle her as I thought it would. She sipped on her tea calmly. Then looked at me.

"Go on!" instead of asking any question she put the ball back in my court.

"I know that Arjun is not Asha Rani's son!"

"What's new in that?" she asked. "Anyone who stays here long enough would know that!"

"What do you mean?" this time I asked for I thought this was classified information.

"My father had an affair with a prostitute! Arjun is the result! These things cannot be hidden for too long especially for a family like ours." She said.

"Does it not bother you this might harm Pratap Singh's image, your image if it gets out!"

"It hasn't got out till now in the media! We have our ways to make sure it doesn't!"

There she was! Coming to the point

"How?" I probed.

"You don't need to know every how!" she said coldly.

"I do need to know! You cannot just say that and not tell me how you make sure it doesn't get out!"

"We have connections Bittu! You already know that! Plus there isn't a soul out there, not that I know of, who will dare to go leak this without any valid proof. I mean we are talking about Pratap Singh and Arjun Pratap Singh!"

"What if someone has valid evidence?"

"You are such a child Bittu!" she rebuked me.

That upset me.

"You think me and Arjun haven't dug into this! I love Arjun to death even if he is my half-brother. I have gone to the end of this world to make sure there are no loose ends. My father made one mistake. He doesn't have to pay all his life for that! There is no evidence. Plus this kind of information is worth a lot. Had anyone had it they would want to extort. No one has tried!"

"You are saying all this to me! What if I go and say this to someone?" I wanted to understand what her game was. Raju's mysterious death kept on coming to my mind. Was that how they made sure things were kept under cover?

"You wouldn't! Your aspirations are different! Let's not forget you have nothing to back it up!" The coldness with which she was talking was unnerving.

"There has been no one ever who didn't like you people at all and had their hands on this? Seems strange!" I probed.

"There was one actually. Not particularly close I would say but Baba was quite close to him!"

My ears perked up.

"Who was this?"

"Not someone I was too familiar with! He was a journalist with a newspaper! He had been following Baba's work for a lot of years. He was obsessed with him." She said.

"What happened to him?"

"He wanted to write a biography on him. But the poor fellow passed away in an accident!"

I wanted to act surprised. I couldn't.

Mallika was observing me closely. She was getting curious and it didn't mean well for me. Had she found out that Mugdha had told me everything, chances were our dead bodies would be found floating in the flood waters.

I had to play tactfully. It was important that I didn't seem too eager. I was perplexed why Mallika was telling me these things so easily. Nine of ten pieces of the puzzle pointed the picture towards her. Was she playing me? Was she trying to find out how much I knew without giving me any important information?

"What accident?" I asked.

"Not too sure. He was run over by a speeding truck!"

Convenient, I thought.

"He had been digging deep with Baba's past and he had come across the fact that Arjun was not born out Baba's marriage with mom!"

"Do you know what did he find out?"

"No! He had mentioned this to Baba, but never handed over any documents as such that would give out these details. I mean he must have gone through some crazy investigation to have found this one. Baba was surprised and he had asked him to keep it under wraps!"

"Which he did not agree to do?" I asked curiously. Of course, he must not have and then paid with his life, I thought.

"Are you saying Raju found out somehow that Arjun was not Asha Rani's son but before he could write the book he died in a road accident?" I continued.

"Sounds fishy, doesn't it?" she said sipping on her tea cup. Mallika's reaction surprised me. Contrary to the belief with which I had walked in her room. Anyone would have believed her and declared her innocent. But I knew her. I knew she was trying to play me.

"Yes it does and I am sure you don't expect me to believe that was just an accident?"

She kept quiet for a minute. She looked at me keenly.

"Are you actually implying what I think you are implying?" she asked, her voice taking a sudden sharp turn. The Mallika route.

"I am just adding the twos and twos here! I am sure no one ever got their hands on the evidence that Raju had found?"

Mallika nodded. *How would they*, I thought, when he was murdered for the same?

"Everyone in this family was ok with a complete stranger finding this out? This never came out, but what if he had handed over whatever he had found to someone else? Are you not scared that this will come out in the wrong way?"

"To be honest everyone was against it! It was Baba's life and no one had the right to make it public. I am glad it never came out. It would not only have had an impact on Baba but would have killed Arjun for sure. He is always under scrutiny. He was under immense pressure at that time for his affair with Maaya. The last thing he would have needed was the press to hound him!"

This was the first time Mallika had mentioned about Maaya to me. She didn't even realise she had said it.

"I am convinced that either Raju had not found anything, it was something he must have heard and was digging around for evidence or if there was any, he never gave it to anyone. If the first one was true, no one has to worry about anything. Also, had he given it to someone, as I said, someone by now would have tried to do something with it."

"Maybe they are waiting for the right time!"

She looked at me.

"Maybe!" she said.

"Until that happens, I'm not going to bother myself with it!" she said.

We both kept quiet for a minute. She was looking a bit more tensed than she was when I had entered the room. Maybe re living the entire episode was what brought the creases on her forehead.

"I know about Maaya's death". I don't know why I was blurting out all this.

She turned towards me.

"Yes it was unfortunate! We never even found her body! It was horrific!"

"Did you like her?" I asked her. I was observing her keenly as she stood near the window now.

"Did I like her?" she laughed.

"Of course I didn't!" she said with an honesty that cut across the distance between me and her.

"Why?" I was again taken aback by her answer. I expected her to lie and pretend she liked her.

"She was an opportunist! She was using Arjun and he was completely blind in her love. He rescued her from that god forsaken place, and the next thing you know, he bought her a house, a car. She was like a leech that was sucking on to his blood." Sheer hatred in her voice!

"Arjun is a good man but he was letting her exploit him. I will agree that she was pretty, and she had her charms. But I am sure charm is what she used to sell! Before we knew it, she was in our house."

"You did not protest?" I asked. I could feel her seething with anger.

"I did not need to. Mom was furious that Arjun got engaged to her. The last thing she needed was another woman of the business to be in the same house as hers. Maaya was lucky mom didn't shoot her!"

This was a new angle. All these time Asha Rani was a mystery to us. Finally Mallika had spoken about her.

"Is she sick now?" I asked trying to be as polite as possible.

"Yes! She had a nervous breakdown when Maaya moved to her house. Since then she has been like this. Quiet!"

Was it possible that Asha Rani was responsible for Maaya's death? Or was it just an accident? That we were reading too much into it.

There was too much unfolding in too little time. My mind was not able to keep up with this. The night, I was convinced that Mallika was responsible for plotting two murders. An hour in her room and I was not too sure anymore. I couldn't decide which was true. Which one was reality? Were these murders or were they just accident? The timing of the two deaths did not go hand in hand. Raju died when he found that Arjun was not who he was, Arjun got engaged to Maaya and Maaya dies in an accident. Asha Rani had a nervous breakdown and has been a walking vegetable since.

I tried to deduct the suspect. Arjun was out of the picture. It was Mallika and Pratap Singh. Or so I thought. They seemed to be the only one who could have had the most interest. They didn't want Raju to publish the book, maybe he didn't listen to them and they had him killed before he could make it public. But the problem did not end there. Arjun got engaged to Maaya, who was not exactly the kind of wife they had hoped for Arjun. Plus she was destructive. Asha Rani's breakdown must have added the final blow and they had her killed. It all seemed to tie up but how was I going to prove it. I looked at Mallika and despite everything holding fort, her way of talking did not corroborate it that they were involved. But was I too believe a woman who's every drop of blood screamed politics?

What had I gotten entangled in? Why did I have to come to know all this? Now I had to find out. I couldn't leave it the way it was, not anymore. I also knew knowing the entire truth could be fatal to me. I thought of pulling the final string on Mallika?

"What happened to the journal?" I asked point blank.

"What journal?" she asked again looking perplexed.

"Maaya's journal!"

Her mouth opened.

"She had a journal?"

"Yes she did and someone in this house has it!"

"I don't have it. Arjun must have had it if he has told you!"

"Arjun did not tell me!" I was walking dangerous territory now. I was this close to betraying Mugdha.

"Then who told you?" I could see that the idea of Maaya keeping a journal and her not knowing about it irked her. It was visible. The very idea of Maaya having written a journal meant she had written things that could have not been good for anyone. I kept quiet. I had said too much.

"Tell me who the hell told you about the journal?" she demanded.

A sudden surge of the blood to my brains! My hands were cold. My back dripping in sweat. My feet were not willing to hold my weight!

"Mugdha?" she asked curiously. I nodded.

She seemed to be thinking something very hard. I looked at her. In her eyes I saw what I had missed.

CHAPTER 30

Mallika paced towards the door and leaned over the wooden railing to see if Arjun was around. He was climbing up the stairs. She gestured to him to come over to her room.

"You don't do the talking!" she demanded of me.

Arjun walked inside the room and Mallika immediately shut the door behind him.

"Did Maaya ever write a journal?" she asked him point blank.

He looked at me, trying to figure out what did I do now.

"Answer me will you?" Mallika was furious.

"Not that I know of!"

"That's not an answer!" she demanded.

"No she didn't!" He said.

"You never came across a red diary that was kept on the table that's on the left side of your bed." I asked.

"I would know had she kept a diary!" he said confidently.

"What are you women up to?" he asked.

Mallika looked at me. The entire story had taken a turn that both I and she tacitly agreed on. We both refrained from spelling it out in front of him. The backlash from him would have thrown everything out of the window.

My heart was refusing to believe the concept that my mind had stated to perceive now. It earnestly hoped that it was wrong. All that i had come to believe in the last few months were about to be shattered in a moment.

"I am going to ask you something, please answer taking your time. It's important!" I said to Arjun

"Why on earth should I answer you?" he said arrogantly.

"Enough with your silliness! Answer the girl!" Mallika said waving her hand towards me.

"Was Mugdha in India in 2001?" I asked.

He opened his mouth to say something, then stopped and thought.

"No! She came to India a few months later!" he said.

"After Maaya passed away?" Mallika asked.

"Yes!" he said.

"What date?"

"Date?" he seemed surprised. He seemed to be having a hard time to understand what was going on.

"Yes date please!" I asked.

"I think it was 21st May!"

My heart broke into pieces.

"Are you sure?" I asked my voice choking. My eyes were filled with tears.

"I picked her up from her house! I am sure! It was our friend Rohan's bday!" he said. Rohan was one of Arjun's school friends. We all knew him. He was one of the few close friends he had.

I sat down on the bed. My head was spinning. I couldn't believe it. I knew I was seeing the entire picture clearly, clearer than ever and anyone. But a part of me just resisted it. All the time I spent knowing someone had my back, all the time I slept in peace knowing I had found a friend, all a lie!

Mallika'e eyes were as wide as mine. She had put the pieces together too.

I had told her that I had seen the dates on Mugdha's passport.

"Do you know if Mugdha maintains a journal?" I asked curiously. I had to sort the matter about the journal. There was more to it.

"Never in her life!" he said. "Although she did have a red diary in her bag!" he said after a pause.

Mallika looked at me.

"Arjun, Mugdha was here in India on 10th Dec 2001 and 15th May 2002, did you know that?" Asked Mallika after Arjun kept on gesturing at him to tell me what was going on.

"What? No! I mean she was definitely not in India in 2001 and she reached Mumbai on 21st May in 2002. What is this about?" he was getting agitated.

This was a difficult situation for both me and Mallika. We didn't have any evidence that would link Mugdha to the every thing directly. To make matters worse, it was Mugdha; the cheerful, happy girl who selflessly stood by Arjun during every crisis of his life. One who loved him so much, it didn't matter to her that he didn't reciprocate the same feelings. She was everyone's darling. She was my best friend.

We were working on a hunch here. But it was clear that she had to have a reason to have lied about her being in India. It would have been a strange co incidence otherwise that Raju died on 15th Dec 2001, five days after her visit to India and Maaya passed away on 16th May, a day after she was in India. Why would she have lied to everyone about her being in India at that time? Did she do it, so that the police wouldn't have reason to suspect her? But she was never part of the interrogation as well. She was always outside the radar of suspects.

"What diary are you talking about?" asked Mallika.

I didn't pay attention to that. I was concentrating so hard to remember every word of our discussion last night.

She asked again.

"Bittu, what is this diary you are talking about?"

Arjun shook my elbow to get my attention.

"Mugdha showed me a few photo copied pages last night which was according to her the copies of Maaya's journal, the red diary she used to maintain. She showed me the entire thing!"

"What bull shit is this? Maaya never maintained a journal and even if did, I would have found it. Of all people Mugdha knows about it and even if there was one and that's the one that I have seen with her, are you implying that Mugdha has lied to me about it?" Arjun was furious. But what he didn't know is by framing the question the way he did, he answered a lot of our questions.

Mugdha had no reason to hide the diary from Arjun and share it with me. Why would she do that? There was only one possible explanation. She wanted me to believe that Maaya was feeling threatened. That's why she had started writing the journal. She wanted me to believe that Mallika was involved in this. She knew I had the itch to take on this family. After I told her about how Harry tricked me, she would have known that it would have given me an enormous advantage to have a number on Mallika. She knew I wanted to find out the dirty about this family so that my lie could be bargained with.

How was I supposed to ever prove this?

Arjun did not understand much what was going on. He sat there for close to an hour trying to be a part of what I and Mallika were talking about. Mallika was cautious how she was letting Arjun in what was being talked about. We were certain that Arjun would think us to be plain crazy, walk out of the room and pour everything out to Mugdha.

As much as I wanted any of it to be not true, I wanted to confront her. There was a definite lack of motif to link her to both the deaths. Even if we considered for argument' sake that she was involved in Maaya's death, there was nothing to link her to Raju's death. Yet time and again, she had lied to everyone about being in India at that time.

Arjun finally lost his patience and got up to walk out of the room.

"Do me one favour Arjun!" said Mallika.

"Don't discuss any of this with her. Trust me on that!" said Mallika. She had a pleading look in her eyes.

We both knew Arjun would not mention anything.

As I sat there explaining Mallika about our discussion the night before, it was clear that Mugdha had planted this story to deviate my attention. The entirety about the diary was a lie but whose journal did she show me?

Then it clicked.

"I think Mugdha showed you her journal. Either that or she has written one just to play it as a trump card!"

"Wouldn't anyone come to know, I mean the handwriting?"

"Bittu, open your eyes! How would you verify a dead woman's hand writing?"

"We need to find a motif!" I said.

"That's what is eluding me!" said Mallika.

As we sat there thinking, I remembered the last pages of the journal. The parts where writing was not clear, the content did not make sense, lucid and hazy! Was there a chance that what Mugdha was portraying as Maaya's state of mind was actually her state of mind? Was there even a tiny possibility that Mugdha's mind was disintegrating and no one knew about it? That all those years of loneliness had made her mind turn a dark corner she couldn't come out of? Was it possible that she hated the Pratap Singh family so much that she wanted to make sure its plagued with doubts and fears?

All these aside, there was one more theory. She wanted Arjun all for herself! She didn't want to share him with anyone, not the family, not with the woman! She was not a raging lunatic at work here and that made her more dangerous.

CHAPTER 31

It was mid-afternoon already and the daylight was scarce. The dark clouds had engulfed the Mumbai skies. We could hear the gurgling of the water level sweeping across the lanes. I walked past Mugdha's room a couple of times to check on her. I was scared to death to be honest. I wanted to run away from all this. Pratap Singh Bhavan looked like the gallows to me. The walls were leaning over to whisper to me. The floors were grabbing onto my feet to stop me from running away. The doors were enticing me to walk inside them so that they could swallow me and the secrets I now held.

The door to her room was locked from inside. I could hear the stereo playing. It was her portable battery operated stereo. I wish life could go back a couple of days when I didn't know all this, when I knew her to be my friend, when I looked up to her as someone as my family. I was angry at myself. I was angry at her. I was once again angry at everything about me.

I saw Mallika walking past her room too. She looked anxious. I observed her closely. Was there a chance she was playing me too? Why did I believe her all of a sudden? I wanted to know the end of it and know once for sure.

In the next hour Mumbai was put on alert. Life had come to a grinding halt. We heard reports on the radio how people were stuck right in the middle of highways, inside cars, how vehicles were floating in the water, how people had climbed up trees to be safe. The water had entered Pratap Singh Bhavan as well. As we all camped on the first floor of the Pratap Singh Bhavan, the ambience had the tinge of a bad mystery novel where something was promising to go wrong any moment but eventually nothing happened. The anticipation was high! With me and Mallika it was not the floods, it was what we needed to do after it subsided. Arjun was occupied with something on his mind; the creases on his forehead didn't lie. Maybe Mallika and me had managed to penetrate his thoughts. Mugdha's room was still closed. I wondered what she was doing. Maybe she was taking a nap.

"We wait for tomorrow!" said Mallika to me obviously noticing that I was pacing outside Mugdha's room.

The evening came and no respite! No electricity! The walls were damp, the house had started stinking. Pratap Singh was getting jittery with all the stench.

Arjun and Harry decided to make soup for everyone. It was heartening to see how they treated the servants of the house. In a time like this when they had to share the same space as the other family members, Arjun realised they were probably as uncomfortable as them. So he went out of his way to make sure they felt at place.

He came over to me and offered me some. He noticed I was looking tensed. He went and knocked on Mugdha's door a few times. No answer. It was strange. I smelled something was fishy.

I went over to Mallika.

"What if she has got a hint that we are up to something?" I asked.

"She won't be able to do anything! She can't leave the house until tomorrow. There is water everywhere!"

It made sense. I was sure she was up to something. She hadn't come out of her room for hours. It was unlike her. If she was trying to plan an escape, that's all the answer I needed.

When the night fell and she still didn't come out of her room, Mallika came over to me.

"We need to keep an eye on her. This is not looking good!"

I looked at Mallika. Every minute she didn't come out of the room, she was getting surer that we were not wrong.

I sat at the corridor. Keeping an eye on the door. My eyes fixed! My mind on those four dates.

10th Dec 2001.15^{th} Dec 2001, 15th May, 16th May 2002!

I was trying to calm myself down to understand what might have been the reason for Mugdha doing all this. Her innocent smile, her bouncy hair, they were there everytime I closed my eyes. How many times I held her hand and told her she was my best friend. How many times she put her arm around me and told me she was there for me! I thought of all the times I saw the longing in her eyes the way she looked at Arjun even on the morning-afters. I couldn't stop the tears. For the first time in my life I had believed someone! Once again, I was the one losing out on something.

A few minutes of silence and I was able to piece it together.

Arjun had known Mugdha since his childhood. She was always in love with him. After Arjun broke off his engagement with her for Maaya, Mugdha tried to be strong and be there for Arjun. That was the only way she could be close to him. Had she broken off ties with him, she would have lost him forever. To whom? To a woman like Maaya! Who had no comparison with her? Yet Arjun loved her more than he could have ever loved Mugdha. Then came Raju in the picture who threatened to take away everything from Arjun by revealing about his parentage. That would have broken him down. She didn't want that. She hated anyone with all her life who wanted to hurt Arjun. She must have come to know about Raju from Arjun. They used to talk everyday. So she came down to India without telling anyone and made sure Raju never had the chance to reveal anything. How she did it was something I needed to figure out. That was just the starting of her problems. Arjun got engaged to Maaya and got her to move to his house. Even Asha Rani's nervous breakdown did not deter him. There was really one way left? Wasn't it? She was about to lose Arjun for good. She came down to India on 15th May 2002 again. Maaya died on 16th May. There was not a possibility that Mugdha didn't have anything to with her death. The fact that she lied to Arjun and made it look like she reached India only on 21st May was the link that connected her to Maaya's death. How she did all this was something yet to be found out. Then she wrote the diary and showed it to me to make it look like that Mallika was involved in this. To turn us against each other! She wanted me out of the house! One way or the other! She couldn't stand knowing Arjun was going to be close again to a woman named Maaya. Yes that was it! She knew once Arjun came to know I had used the name, somehow he would start looking for her in me. She couldn't take that chance anymore, could she?

These crazy theories nesting in my head, next thing I knew I could feel something cold against my face. I had fallen asleep. My face was on the floor. I could see that the faint light of the dawn was peeping across the lawn. I woke up with a start. I saw that people were still sleeping in the hall across. Mugdha's room was still closed.

I got up to see where Mallika was! I saw that she was standing across the hall staring at the backyard.

I went over to her. She was looking at the garage.

"I fell asleep!" I said.

"I did too!" she said looking at the door. I leaned over to take a look. The garage door was open and one of the cars was missing. I ran over to Mugdha's room. It was still locked from inside.

"The door is still locked from inside!" I said to her.

"I know! The bitch must have jumped out of the balcony!"

"Fuck! The balcony!" I had completely missed there was a balcony in her room.

"When did you notice?" I asked her.

"I got up half an hour back. I remembered about the balcony and that it faces the garage! I came over and there it was!"

"You know what that means?" I asked her.

"Yes! She must have heard us yesterday!"

"What do we do? Call the police?" I asked.

"No! Arjun wouldn't believe us! It would kill him. Lets not change the story for him!"

"We can't let her go just like that, can we?"

"We can! We don't have anything on her! No concrete evidence. Its up to her to explain to Arjun why she vanished like this!"

"Should we call her parents?" I asked. I was clearly not paying attention to what she was saying.

"Bittu! She is gone! For good! We can't do anything! We have nothing on her! Not the diary, not the passport! Even if we get the police involved, its my brother who is hurting at the end of the day"

Mallika knew Mugdha was involved in the deaths. But did it make her any sad apart from the fact she was wrong about her, like everyone else? I don't think so.

"She did it for Arjun! But she wont come back knowing I know now!" said Mallika.

The fact that Mallika was trying to reason was enough for me to understand this secret would die with us.

"You wont say anything to Arjun! Its his life! Don't hurt him anymore. He will not know to trust anymore."

Maybe she was right. He didn't need to know this. Mugdha didn't harm him. Maybe there was more to Maaya than we knew. Maybe she saw it.

"Not sure about Raju, but I am happy she got rid of Maaya, if she did it!" said Mallika, her old calm self back.

"What?"

"heard me right! She was duping Arjun. Everyone could see except for him! All for the good I say!" she walked away.

As I stood there, it occurred to me, life didn't matter to these people. Did it not have any value? Mugdha most probably had committed a serious crime; no matter how horrible a person Maaya was, no one had the right to decide her life, to decide for Arjun. The only other person who who was able to solve the puzzle was glad it happened. I was part of it now. It was going to be the beginning of countless sleepless nights for me. For a fear had begun to settle in. The fear of being watched! The fear of my life.

* * *

CHAPTER 32

Slowly the days rolled by. Pratap Singh Bhavan had come to a standstill much like the rest of the city for the first couple of days. But the beauty about this city is the spirit of its people. Cities make people and people make cities! To get back on its feet, Mumbai never needs a push. It gets up and starts moving. So did the members of Pratap Singh Bhavan.

The floods not only damaged the house—the rain had damaged the paint of the house, it was a poor mixture of green and brown, the lawn was a wreck. We even had to move the carcass of a few dead animals. An electric pole lay on the ground diagonally across the house and anyone wanting to go out had to jump over it at the risk of stepping on it and electrocuting themselves. The servant's quarter was now a skeleton remains. But where there was visible damage to property, there was an unspoken loss of relationships. Mugdha's sudden disappearance had a profound impact on me. I couldn't eat for days. Every night I would be awake. Thinking of whether I was wrong, whether I was tricked. My heart wept like it had wept for nothing. I had lost the will to do anything. More than anything else, it was the loss of a friend from my life. The empty feeling in my chest was like a huge black hole sucking in everything without a trace. The loneliness that enveloped my life was beyond words. Above all, the idea of my trust being broken again was hard to get over.

As for Arjun, he didn't realise what had happened. He thought she had gone to her father's house. But when he didn't hear back from her for the whole week, he went over to their house and came to know she had been there to meet them only once. She had informed she was going back to U.S. He tried calling her but without any luck. He was unhappy that she had left without a message but then later I heard him telling Mallika that it was typical of her. She hated good byes. That day I felt sad for her. No matter what, her love for Arjun was true. She had loved him with everything. She could have chosen anyone but she chose him. She stuck with him. In his highs and lows, made his tragedies personal, made his happiness her reason to live! She never complained; never shed a tear in front of anyone. She knew only one thing. To make him happy! She had given him her everything. She was different from any woman I had met in my life. Yet she was the same as any! When she loved, she loved with the raging passion only a woman can love with.

The man didn't even realise how he turned someone into something else. I hated Arjun for that. He drove her to this extent, didn't even have a clue. He was the reason the woman who had with an open heart accepted him, was limited to the confines of the house. Somehow I thought he was responsible for her Maaya's death.

There is no dark cloud without a silver lining though. A few days later, time had come for me to move out of Pratap Singh Bhavan. The night before leaving for the show, I prayed. I prayed that no matter what happened I didn't have to come back to this house.

No one shed a tear the morning I left. No one hugged me as I left. Mallika wished me the best; Pratap Singh didn't notice anything different. Arjun was his usual indifferent self. Asha Rani still didn't bother. But it was Harry who drove me there. I could see that his way of looking at me had changed. He was far more polite and less cheeky than before. I didn't know at that time though if I could ever look at him any different than I did.

This was the starting of a long journey for me. As I stepped out of the house and into the world to find my feet once again I knew I had to guard myself. For the ways of the world won't change to accommodate me, I had to change to fit into it! This was the end of the road for Bittu and Maaya was set to be back again!

*   *   *

I shed Bittu from my life. Her clothes, her way of talking, her way of smiling, her way of letting people treat her! Maaya was born on the show! The transformation from a simple girl who didn't have the slightest clue how to dress herself was something the channel cashed in on! They made my make over the agenda of the show! People wanted to see me as I represented the dreams of many a gawky, and ugly girls out there. Viewership went high as not only I was outshining others in singing, but the drama I was able to create was unimaginable. From crying on the camera because I felt too nervous to fainting in the middle of a song, to an image make over to an indication of a scandalous affair with one of the contestants on the show, everything was being lapped up by the audience. A bit of originality, a lot of lies with a twist of scripting! Eight weeks of Maaya was not enough! I lost out in the final four but was brought back due to public demand as the viewership dropped a bomb on my exit.

The day the first episode aired on tv, Arjun Pratap Singh was waiting outside the studio. He stood in a corner by his car watching me closely as I crossed the road. I was afraid that he would come and hit me for he had now found out I was using Maaya's name. But no! He just stood there watching me. When he did this for the next 5 days, it was drove me mad. I expected him to come and talk to me. But he didn't! I hated that. So finally one day, when he stood in his brooding shadow, smoking a cigarette, I walked up to him to confront him.

"What the hell is wrong with you?" I asked. He said nothing.

I stared back at him, angry at him. The anger had not subsided. I wanted to hit him.

"Will you talk?" I asked again. He still didn't say anything. By this time, I had lost my patience. I had to somehow vent my anger.

I slapped him across his face. So hard it made a clapping sound. He didn't budge. "I missed you!" was all he said as I climbed into his car and drove off.

That night something had happened. The tension between us was back again! The spark re-ignited! Either it was sheer hatred that made my blood boil or it was the intense attraction I felt towards him. Whatever it was I knew he was feeling the same thing.

I went on to be the runner up on the show. I hated it that I didn't win. I hated the girl who won it. I made my resentment for her public when I refused to congratulate her. But all was not lost for me. The girl who left Kanpur's Ranipur Society was now a popular face on television. People identified me wherever I went. The sheer pleasure it gave me, the boost my ego got when someone asked for my autograph was overwhelming. I wished I could see those faces back home who had snubbed me all these years. There was a vengeance taking over me that wanted to prove to them that how worthless their limited life was. I wanted to throw the money at Lala's face and tell him to go fuck off along with his wife and daughter. I took up any contract that came my way. From singing for live shows to recording for songs in other languages! I didn't mind as long as the money was coming. Each night I would open my grandmom's jewellery box and stare at it, knowing I wasn't far from what I wanted from life.

The next couple of years went by in a flash. My efforts to reconcile with my family was limited to one attempt when I tried to call them up but my father hung up on me saying Bitty Kumari had passed away a few years back. I felt sad in the beginning but I had come to not worry about it anymore. There was something that had slowly developed in my life.

My proximity to Arjun! The fear that had begun to settle in me when Mugdha left was starting to surface slowly. I felt being watched all the time. Every time a truck would pass I would be shaking with fear. Every time I was on the highway, I could see blood. I trembled with fear when I imagined Mugdha's face, smiling; knowing that I was privy to her secret now. I could feel her satisfaction when my heart raced faster knowing she was still out there, hiding somewhere, mingled in the crowd. Those wide eyes following me!

Would she be in peace? Not a chance in hell. But I was not the one who would let the fear take control of my life. Each passing day, I was convinced I wanted to teach her a lesson for playing me. The cunning in me was waiting to surface again!

I got my chance soon. Arjun and I were seeing each other regularly since that night a year ago when I slapped him. He used to frequent my place quite often and despite the obvious inclinations for each other we had not expressed anything. Then one night tired of all the games, I kissed him. I didn't expect resistance. But I didn't expect the fierce response. He kissed me like he had no tomorrow. We were so carried away in that moment that we didn't get the chance to go from the living room to the bedroom. The rug on the living room was to be thankful for!

A woman never forgets her first they say. Arjun was not my first. But I didn't want to consider Harry as my first. I wanted to live in denial! At least Arjun was the first since that night. The connection I felt shook me to my bones and I knew this was something I didn't want to give up. Arjun was falling for me, the remote connection I had with Maaya was something he couldn't resist. I knew if Mugdha was keeping a watch, she would know this. Nothing would hurt her than this. Knowing I was taking away her reason to live! She had to pay, I was making her!

* * *

<u>Year 2011</u>

15th May 2011, my wedding day! I was once again back in Pratap Singh Bhavan! This time as Arjun Pratap Singh's wife! It was like a dream come true. The long fleet of expensive cars, the celebrity guest list. The unbridled show of lavish, luxury and money! My honeymoon planned—a trip across Europe.

I was dressed so splendidly that men and women had their jaws dropping to the ground at the same time. I saw myself in the mirror and couldn't recognise myself.

I was grinning so hard that my face was hurting after the wedding was over. Then I saw Mallika standing at one corner nursing her drink. Despite the unspoken and tacit nature of our initially sour relationship, she had been supportive of my alliance with Arjun. The beholding of Mugdha's secret between the two of us brought us closer. We both shared our fear. Mallika was nothing like me but it was evident not knowing Mugdha's where about disturbed her. I noticed she was looking pale. The colour of her face had vanished. I walked towards her, I realised she was sweating. I could sense something was wrong. I picked up my wedding dress, the little stars on the *lehenga* making a clattering nose. I tapped her on her shoulder. She was startled and dropped her glass.

"Mallika, are you all right? "I asked. She turned towards me.

Beads of sweat trickling down her neck! Her hands were trembling. She turned around and was looking at the piano kept at the corner. I could hear it playing. I couldn't see who it was! The crowd had gathered around there blocking the view.

I went over, moving between the guests. They saw me and allowed me inside. Arjun was there smiling at whoever was playing the piano!

I could see the back of the woman playing the piano. Dressed in a resplendent white gown, impeccable figure, long straight hair flowing down her shoulder. She was playing the piano with amazing finesse. I walked around the piano to be able to see who she was. To be face to face with her!

Our eyes met and my heart stopped. The broad smile of her's pierced through me, as if someone had shot me. The curls were gone. The smile had not.

It was Mugdha.

I kept on looking at her. She kept her eyes on me. The piercing eyes and the cheerful smile! She puckered her lips to give me flying kiss.

Then a man held her by the shoulder, kissed her on the cheek! She kissed him back. I noticed he was a young man. Well dressed, hair neatly kept and a striking resemblance to someone I knew years back.

I looked at him closely. The more I looked at him, the more I felt I was living my worst nightmare.

It was my brother! It was Dev!

AUTHOR'S NOTE

All the characters in the book have no resemblance to any one in real life. This is purely a work of fiction and any similarities to any one and any situation is purely co-incidental.